AFTER C
VERBAL WARNING

A NOVEL BY

RYAN BRACHA

© Copyright Ryan Bracha 2016

Abrachadabra Books
in association with

Paddy's Daddy Publishing

All rights reserved. No part of this publication may be reproduced or transmitted in any form or by any means without permission of the author.

All the characters in this book are fictitious and any resemblance to actual persons, living or dead, is purely coincidental. You know this is bullshit, right?

Also by Ryan Bracha

Strangers Are Just Friends you Haven't Killed Yet

Tomorrow's Chip Paper

The Banjo String Snapped But The Band Played On

Bogies, and other equally messed up tales of love, lust, drugs and grandad porn

Paul Carter is a Dead Man

Twelve Mad Men

Ben Turner is a Dead Man

The Switched

Davie Craig is a Dead Man

This, and each of the three books that will succeed it in the After Call Work series, are based on a true story. They are based on a million true stories. And some lies.

For those of you who have not yet wised up.

Verbal Warning

THURSDAY

After Call Work

Chapter One

Barry

It's my scheduled dinner time in four minutes and I've been available to take a call for a minute. If I'm lucky I might make it to half twelve without taking another one as it's been very quiet today, thankfully.

"What's for dinner, Fat Fuck? A bucket of salad and a gallon of low fat jelly?" A hushed and malicious voice asks. Steven. I hate Steven. He's very mean to me. I take out my notebook and I write his hurtful comments down under the eight different things he's already said to me today. He grins at me and then his mouth opens.

"Darren! Barry's got his notebook out again, supposed to be a paperless environment," he states. God, I hate him.

Our team leader's head pops up from his computer and looks accusingly at me.

"What have I told you about that? If Bev does me for compliance I'm having your balls, mate. Put it away," he says, his head disappearing back behind the computer screen, "Stevie, you're next for a call, mate."

Steven winks and slithers away from me as I put my book away. I'm already on a stage one warning because of him telling on me for having my book out. I've been to HR about him though, when he had a drink of my pop out of the canteen fridge, but they never do anything. Drinking my pop is technically theft and as such he should be done for gross misconduct. It's in all the company policies. No, they never do anything about him. He writes something on

Verbal Warning

his little whiteboard and slides it across. Fat cunt. I try to grab at it but he's too quick. The writing is gone. He logs off of his telephone for lunch and it's only twelve twenty eight. I go to protest but at that exact moment a call comes through. The call that Steven should have taken. The voice on the other end of the line doesn't let me finish. Instead it barks at me that I personally am responsible for its mother's death. I was the one who let the debt build up and I was the one who failed to notify her. I was the one who drove her to suicide. The voice wants to know what I'm going to do about it. I try to speak again but the voice cuts me off again. I watch as the clock hits twelve thirty. I look up to see Steven walking off the call floor, his hand pawing at the bum of Kimberley, the eighteen year old who dances on a night. He's such a sleaze. He claims to have slept with most of the beautiful girls who work here, but they still let him touch them inappropriately. It's offensive and degrading to women. I've been to HR about that too but they've done nothing. The voice swears at me.

"Please don't use that kind of language or I will have to release the call," I say. The voice asks me who I think I am and demands to speak to my manager. No. This means I'm going to be stuck with this for at least thirty more minutes before I can take my lunch. Darren will be angry with me and we'll have to go through my records. This is the fourth escalated call I've given to him already today. I ask the voice to please hold, and I press the button to action that request with a trembling finger.

"Ehm, Darren," I say, taking off my headset. Our eyes meet and I can tell he hates me. That something in his look that's asking what now and I shrug and say sorry. I have an escalation. He asks what I've done and I say I've done nothing. I couldn't even get the account number and they were swearing at me. I warned them not to swear. He mutters something under his breath. I wish I could hear what it was so I could get it in my notebook but I can't. He stands and comes to take the call from me. He tells the voice he's very sorry for its loss. He tells the voice that he'll look into it. He looks directly into my eye when he tells the voice that it will be fed back and dealt with internally. I can't believe this. I didn't do anything wrong. He talks to the voice some more and ten minutes later he has my file open. He's telling me that I'm becoming a lost cause. He's tried to coach me but my objection handling skills are non-existent. He asks if this is really the best place for me.

"I love my job," I lie, "besides, is that really the way a manager should speak to his staff? What would HR say?"

He burns into me with a look of raw hatred.

"Don't threaten me, Barry," he says, and smiles suddenly, "I'm putting you with Steve. You could learn a lot from him."

"What do you mean?" I ask. This can't be happening. Steven is a bully and I can't learn anything from him.

"I mean I want him to mentor you. You need to grow some bollocks when it comes to dealing with customers. Simple as that." Once again I wish I could get my notebook out. A manager shouldn't swear at their staff. It's unprofessional. "How many escalated calls have I taken from you this month, do you think?" I shrug. Nothing I say means anything to him.

Verbal Warning

"Go on," he says, his hand moving the cursor around on the screen to open up a spreadsheet, "have a guess."
"I don't know. Twenty?"
He laughs sarcastically and shakes his head.
"I wish it were twenty. Twenty would be an improvement. You've given me sixty four, Barry. In three fucking weeks. I might as well be sat in your seat doing the job permanently, I'm in it that much. Now how many has Steve given me? Have a guess."
I feel so tiny. So patronised.
"Ten?" I almost whisper.
"None. You know how I know that, without looking?"
I don't say anything. I want to cry. I can feel my cheeks twitching but I hold it back. It only gives them more ammunition. I shake my head.
"Because he's never had an escalated call, mate. I daren't look at your year to date numbers. I'm putting you with Steve because there's questions being asked. It's starting to look like I'm not doing my job, managing it. I'm not gonna lose my job over a slack cunt who can't do his. Do you understand?"
I look at my hands. They're shaking. This is so unfair but I can't do anything about it.
"I asked if you understood, Barry."
I nod.
"Good. Now go and get your dinner. You can sit with him this afternoon."
I feel dizzy as I stand up and go to my desk to log off for lunch. This isn't happening. I hate hate hate Steven more than anything. It's like Darren is trying to force me to leave. I walk slowly from the call floor, passing dozens of other Stevens in the sales teams. Men in

After Call Work

vests, with stupid big muscles. Girls with their boobs half out and lipstick redder than blood. They all break the rules but nobody cares, because they're popular and attractive to each other. The company dress code policy clearly states that business dress should be worn on a Monday to Thursday. HR just tell me to see my manager about it. The door to the canteen opens and there's Steven. He catches my eye and smiles as he holds the door open for me to pass. I mutter a small thanks, but then he burps and catches the air in his cheeks. He then blows it right into my face. It smells of cigarettes and garlic and makes my stomach turn.
"I don't know what it was, mate, but it was delicious. My compliments to the chef," he says as he turns and walks to the call floor. I scoop my hand into my pocket to count up the change as I approach the canteen fridge. I open the door and my suspicions are correct. Where I had left my chargrilled garlic chicken salad there is my empty clear plastic lunchbox. I want to cry. Why doesn't anybody do anything about this? With tears in my eyes I count up my change. Eighty pence. I buy a bag of crisps and I move to the corner of the canteen to eat them. They don't fill even the smallest corner of my stomach. I should complain. I should report him to HR. This is bullying, plain and simple. I will. I stand and I grab my empty salad box and I leave the canteen. Somebody says hello to me in the corridor but I don't know who it is. She's on our contract but not my team. I don't say hello back because I'll cry, I'm that annoyed. And hungry. I stand at the door to HR and my hand comes up and I'm about to knock but I catch Diane's eye. She looks at me from the office in irritation and says something to one

Verbal Warning

of the other HR ladies, she's pretty new but I know her name as Yvonne. They both laugh in derision before Diane beckons me in. They won't take it seriously. I shake my head and walk away. There's no point. I'm on my own. I head for the toilets and I'm about to push open the door.
"Sorry love, you can't use that one," says one of the cleaners from behind me, "we're just about to clean it."
"I just need a wee," I protest, but she's shaking her head.
"Sorry love, you'll have to use the ones over the other side of the building."
I sigh. I really hate my life. I feel the tickle of tears on my cheeks, and I sniff up hard and wipe my eyes and walk away quickly. She laughs with the other cleaning woman and their cackling cuts into me as it echoes behind me. I avoid everyone and everything as I head to the other toilets and lock myself into a cubicle, and I cry, and I cry. I'm starving and annoyed and I have to sit with that massive idiot Steven when I get back. My mentor, the thief. On my seat in the cubicle I look down at my feet. My laces. No. That would mean they win. All of them. All of them. I'm so alone. My shoes are off and I'm picking the laces out. I tie them together and make a loop at one end that I hook over my head and around my neck. My eyes scan the cubicle and find the coat hook on the back of the door. I snare the other end of the laces around it and I watch the thin material stretch from my neck to the hook. I spin around twice, slowly, to tighten it. Then with my back to the door I let my legs give way. The cord bites

After Call Work

into my skin and my throat is tight. This will show all of them. My blood is on their hands.

Verbal Warning

Chapter Two

Penny

He's holding the paper in front of him and reading whatever crap they want us to know, but I'm not listening. I look at my watch, just after one. Three and a half hours to go until I blow this popsicle stand and that's me for the weekend. It's my Friday, bitches! This thing here, a rare team brief. Almost as rare as the lesser spotted coaching session. We're supposed to get an hour a week. Lucky if we get that in a month, and even if we do he never says anything of worth. Just makes his lips flap about stats and then always brings it round to himself, which would be fine if he weren't such a wannabe cool cunt. He's about forty but acts like he's twenty. Always bringing stories up about birds he's shagged and drugs he's popped, but he's been married for like forever. It's bare embarrassing. You know he'd cheat on his wife if only he got the chance. No chance, Jimbo. I'm probably being unfair, he's actually alright compared to some of the other pricks here. Always on the lookout to bust somebody for having their phone out or drinking out of, wait for it, a can. Then they can drag you off to an investigation and cut you loose. They'd rather sack you for one wrongdoing than actually deal with you and make you good at your job. What's that saying though? Pay peanuts and you're getting nothing but fucking monkeys. Something like that. It's mostly a bunch of jobsworth wankers who got their noses brown enough to make the step up to deal with people badly. At least Jimmy here halfway sounds like he

cares. You should hear him on manager calls. Smooth as John Legend holding a glass of Bailey's on a velvet pillow. Then he's off the call and calling the customers all the cunts under the sun. He's still reading the brief from the sheet when Darren Perry comes over from the Team Nine desks. He's looking in a bad way. Worry on his face like he's holding a fart in that he's convinced is gonna be a shit. He hovers about behind me, trying to get Jimbo's attention, which does happen eventually.
"What's up, Daz?" Jimmy asks.
"We've, ehm, got a bit of a situation. First aid, like."
Darren dances about behind me, it's bare irritating. I give him the shit eye but he's not looking. Waste of a good shit eye, that.
"Where's Euan?"
"He's already there. It's urgent. Come on."
Then Jimmy passes the brief to me and tells me to finish reading from where he stopped. He disappears in the direction of the bogs and the rest of the team look at me, half in expectation and half in amusement. The paper says something about call floor standards. Fuck's sake. I look at Danny at the side of me.
"Where we at? Were you listening to him?" I ask. He shrugs.
"Dunno mate," he says. I roll my eyes and put the sheet of paper in his hand.
"I'm not reading it out," I say, "you do it."
He laughs and passes it round to Amber. She passes it to Steph who passes it to Suzy. Eventually it gets round to Tony who it looks like was itching to get his hands on it. He clears his throat and starts talking. Straight away I switch off and I'm wondering what I'm

gonna wear tonight. Maybe the blue Ted Baker dress. It goes with my Michael Kors watch that my mum got me for my eighteenth. It's me and Amber and Suzy off out in town later. Last Thursday of the month, we're out, without fail. That Stevie off Team Nine says he's off out tonight too, so that might be interesting. He's a slimeball. You can't have a proper conversation with him without it coming back round to when you're gonna let him do whatever to you, but I dunno, there's something about him. He's got something going on behind the eyes that intrigues me. I heard he'd shagged Zena, the manager, now she hates him. I heard her calling him all the cunts under the sun in the canteen the other day. It's like she wants to spit every time she says his name. She should have known what he's like. It was never going to be a long term thing with somebody like Stevie. If you climb into bed with him and expect anything more than a good time then you've only got yourself to blame when you don't even get that. It's got to be embarrassing for her, cause he's telling anybody that'll listen that they've done it. She's a manager, too. You've got to have a bit of professionalism when you have a position of authority, have you not? I think you do. If Jimbo had managed to get in my pants then questions would be asked. He's never getting into my pants, by the way. He's like forty and I'm nineteen. Don't bother skipping on for the filthy stuff, it doesn't happen. Just stay here with me and take your time. Anyway, my point is that if you're a manager then you can't be shagging the skivvies.

"Penny?" Tony drags me out of my daydream. I focus on his face, he expects me to answer a question.

After Call Work

"Uh, sorry what?"
His face goes all serious and annoyed.
"Were you even listening?"
"Clearly not, Tony. What do you want?"
He sighs, looking round the team as if to get some back up, but he gets none. Amber and Suzy are chuckling. It's bare funny.
"I asked if you understood what would happen if we lost the accreditation for floor standards," he says, "do you?"
"Not a clue, mate," I say with a shrug, "are we done?" Amber and Suzy are blatantly laughing their arses off now. Tony is bare annoyed.
"Well, no, we're not done. If we lose the accreditation we lose our jobs, love," he says to me like I'm thick or something.
"Uh, excuse me, right. Don't call me love, you hardly even know me, alright? I'll knock you out." I snap. I'm not having him talk to me like shit. The circle of the team goes quiet, except for Amber still squeaking with a laugh she's trying to hold in. Tony looks at me, red faced. You can tell he's gagging to say something to me.
"You're not my manager, Tony, however much you want to be. You can grass as many people up for looking at Facebook as you want but you're still just a brown nosing cunt who earns the same as me. Wind your neck in."
I storm off and leave him to it. He's bare raging too. I go past my desk and straight to the toilet. We've got about ten minutes of the brief left and I'm definitely not spending them on the phone. They might call it avoidance but I call it wanker tax. It's the name of the

Verbal Warning

game. You find as many different ways to not do your job as you can in this place. Take five extra minutes to write your notes up instead of when you're on the call, you've earned it for having to listen to some old woman tell you about her dead pets for the last hour, and watch your scheduled break time (along with your mates) come and go. Be a little bit narky or thick on the call now and then so they ask for your manager. I guarantee it'll buy you twenty minutes of talking to Suzy while he's trying to talk the angry customer down. There's a hundred different ways to not do your job. You just have to know how to do it. Anyway, I'm sorry, I got side-tracked. I'm in the toilet freshening up, and I hear some commotion outside. I open the door and there's big Barry walking along slowly between Euan and Jim who are holding him up. Barry hasn't got his shoes on, because Darren Perry's holding them in one hand, and some string or something in the other. Barry's rubbing his neck and muttering something about being sorry, about just wanting it all to stop. Jim shushes him and tells him it'll be alright, he smiles at me, then they're away through the doors onto the call floor. I've no idea what that was about, but big Barry looked in a bad way. He's harmless. Barry, I mean. I mean yeah, he's an ever bigger grass than Tony, but I'm not sure he's all there, if you get me? He talks to himself and spits when he does it. He's always on a diet but between the salads there's always four empty crisp packets on his desk. Danny calls him Sprinkle, as in he's got a sprinkle of the retarded about him, which is really mean, but I laughed my arse off when he first said it. I go back through to the call floor and see Jim and them

After Call Work

going over to Patrick's desk. They sit Barry down and are all having a chat with Patrick. They call Tara from scheduling over and she's shaking her head. Tara's the one who authorises everybody's holidays and time off and all that. She's a proper dick, her and her sidekick, Curt. Always saying no to time off when you've actually got holidays booked. Patrick looks at everybody and shrugs. Looks at his watch. Shrugs again. Stands up and he's gone. Tara shrugs and goes back to her desk. Euan shrugs and goes to his team. Jimmy shrugs and heads over to our bank of desks. Barry's looking desperately at Darren Perry. What does Darren do? Course he does. He shrugs and hands Barry his shoes and then points to his team. There's no hours available. Whatever's up with Barry, he's going to have to put up with it. Honestly, you could have your arms and legs dangling off and Tara would still make you go back and carry on if there was no availability. No wonder so many phone in sick.

About ten minutes later the news has travelled all the way round the call floor. Barry tried to kill himself. Tried to hang himself with his shoe laces. Let's be fair, you've got to be in a pretty bad way to get that far. The poor dumb bastard. Now he's got to suffer the rest of his shift knowing that everybody else knows what he did. That's bare embarrassing. If it were me I wouldn't give a fuck, I'd be out of those doors quicker than you could say Samaritans Helpline.

Verbal Warning

Chapter Three

Barry

My belly hurts from being hungry. My eyes hurt from crying. My neck hurts really bad from. You know. Everybody knows. My brain hurts from listening to Steven talk to customers like they're idiots and get away with it. I don't hear the words, just his tone. I feel ashamed. I feel sick. Darren has given me time to, how did he put it? Sort my head out? He says there's no rush to get online, just take my time. Thanks a lot, Saint Darren. He's acting like he's my best friend all of a sudden. It doesn't work that way.
"What did you try to kill yourself for, Fat Fuck?"
I ignore him. I try to ignore him.
"You should've used better laces. Nobody ever hung themselves on George at Asda. You need quality laces."
I try to ignore him. I try so hard.
"Or your belt. I'm sure it's long enough."
I put my headset on and I press ready to take a call. The tone beeps and I introduce myself. The voice gives me its account number and I go into the security questions. We call that passing DPA. The voice gives me its full name. But it says Jake Kilner instead of Jacob Kilner. I tell the voice that I'm afraid I cannot complete the call or give any account information because it didn't give the correct name as it shows on the account. The voice asks me what name I have. I say I'm sorry. I say I cannot give that information. The voice is incredulous. Calls me a jobsworth and tells me the account belongs to the voice. It tells me that if my

After Call Work

company were looking for money it wouldn't be so difficult to access the account. I say, I'm sorry. I don't make the rules. The voice laughs and asks me if I enjoy this little bit of power I have. Asks me if telling people no turns me on. The voice calls me pathetic and tells me again to tell it the name on the account. Tells me it pays my wages and that the customer is always right. The voice laughs again and calls me a fucking pathetic jobsworth virgin cunt. I try to speak but the line goes dead. I want to tell Darren to listen to the call but there's no point. He won't do anything. He'll tell me I could have handled it better. It was my fault. Without realising I've done it I've got my notebook on my desk. I look at Steven who's on a call, and back to the account details. I scribble down Jake Kilner and the address, and put my book away. I look around again to check that nobody saw me. I think I'm okay. I close down the account without accessing it fully. By the time my shift is done there are six more names and addresses in my notebook.

As I walk to the coat rack people look up me from their stations. Dozens of faces staring at me. I know what's going through their minds. There he is. The lad that tried to kill himself. Couldn't even do that right. What a big fat stupid loser. When I look at any of them they turn away. Suddenly talking to their customers again. Their few seconds of morbid rubbernecking at the walking suicide attempt done. They have jobs to do. I get to my leather jacket, the one that my dad gave me, and slide my arms into it.
"Fuckin hell, John Travolta let himself go," says Steven to a girl who I see around but don't know the name of.

Verbal Warning

She's pretty. I don't say anything, I just go red. He's said the same insult before, many times. He says it every time there's somebody different to hear it. I hear it each time he does it. The girl looks at me with pity in her beautiful eyes and then at Steven.
"Leave him alone, Stevie," she says then looks back to me, "I heard what happened. That's bare rough that Tara didn't let you go home. You need to get help, mate."
She tells Steven that she might see him in town later and walks off, giving me the kind of look you'd give a dog that needed putting down. She was nice to me. She was actually kind of nice to me. I smile at her back as she goes, grateful to her.
"Get your eyes off, Fat Fuck. Penny's mine. If you're lucky I might let you smell her on my dick tomorrow."
I don't say anything. I just walk off. He won't win.

At the security turnstiles I wait to leave the building, but it looks like half of the staff in the place have been out for cigarettes and are coming back in, because there are queues at both gates. I stand hopefully looking at every person who approaches, willing them to let me through but they don't. More people join the end of the queues. My bus is due any minute, too. I hover my card over the swipe thing but nobody takes the hint. Still they spin selfishly through the turnstiles and it's not until a loud harsh voice barks out that it stops.
"Bazza, grow some balls and get through that turnstile." Steven. As usual.
I turn to see that a large queue has formed behind me. I look desperately at the people on the other side. An

After Call Work

Asian girl pauses, looks at me and scowls. I apologise quietly as I move through, avoiding looking directly at her, but cannot help feeling relieved when the fresh air hits me as the door to the building opens.

On the bus, I'm lucky enough to get a window seat near the front. I stare out to the industrial estates and businesses of this part of town and I think about today. About what I did and why. About Steven. I hate him so much. It's like he can say and do anything and nobody even blinks. How can they not see what he is? They didn't ask me why. Why I did what I did, I mean. Or, I suppose, what I tried to do. Not one single person in that building actually cares even a tiny bit about me as a person. If I'd died they would have only mourned eight hours a day of service level impact. The loss of one FTE. My headstone would carry nothing more than the words Here lies Barry. He was one Full Time Equivalent. This is only part of what I hate about the place. I could fill a whole novel with what I really despise about it. The people. The people I work for, the people I work with, the customers. I'm not smart enough though, I don't have the imagination. Maybe one day, but not yet. I pull out my notebook and pen, and I write down the things that Steven and Darren said to me today. I write down what I did. What I tried to do. The book is almost filled already. It's 160 pages of nasty things said to me; insults and names. Thefts. Broken rules and ignored policies. I started keeping it earlier this year, after I Googled bullying in the workplace when HR ignored my complaints yet again. The website said to keep a log of everything, as some sort of evidence, so I did. The thing with Steven is that

Verbal Warning

he's sly. He always makes sure to call me by my name and make everything sound light-hearted when anybody else is around. When nobody can hear him he says really mean things. Things only I hear. Still, I write them down and eventually one day he will get what's coming to him.

The house I live in has five other occupants. For the most part, we don't know each other, it's just that we all share the bathroom, lounge and kitchen, and each rent a room. It's cheap, and all the bills are included in the rent. It's not ideal, but it's a roof over my head. You can learn to plan your meals around three Polish warehouse packers, a drug addict who hates you, and an author who continually pushes his books at you. His favourite line is Hi, I'm Allen Inches, that's I.N.C.H.E.S, I write books, find me at all good online book stores and he thinks it's really funny but it's really not. He shouts things out at night. His room is above mine. You can learn to clean yourself in five minutes. You can train your bladder to be ready at a second's notice if you hear the bathroom light click off. You can learn your lesson first time when you make the landlord aware that there's a weird smoky smell coming from the drug addict's room and you think it might be marijuana. When the drug addict does a poo in your washing and swears at you and threatens to murder you. That's the exact point in your life that you can make a decision to not be interested in that man at all. You can live with the horrible pickle smell that clings to everything in the house from whatever the Polish are cooking and eating at seven every other morning. These are the things that eventually get used

After Call Work

to. With intense and relentless conditioning you can ignore almost anything. There are cracks though. Steven. My employers. Customers. As I unlock the door to my room I pull out my notebook and flick past the insults, and the stealing, and find the page with the names in. The addresses. I pull out my laptop from beneath my two seater sofa and get the social medias up. I find Jake Kilner quite easily. He's got no privacy settings on so I look at his photographs from a stag party in Magaluf. He has a tattoo of a large cross on his back. His daughter is called Lily May. He supports his local football team. He listens to rap music. He lives in the next town. He likes to try to connect with celebrities a lot on Twitter. He has a dating profile but he has a relationship status as engaged. He's not a nice man. I put the auto fill settings to Jake Kilner's details and I apply for credit cards, loans, spam mail, free samples, sexual health material, porn magazines and emails. For each new idea I have, it hits a rich vein of other possibilities. I move quickly around the Internet until I have signed Jake Kilner up for every mailing list that there is, and it's gone three in the morning by the time I'm done. I was supposed to be healing a dungeon raid on World of Warcraft tonight, too. I've got some apologies to make tomorrow. It's my day off tomorrow, I can catch it up then.

Verbal Warning

Chapter Four

Penny

I'm on my second glass of Prosecco by the time Amber gets here from hers. We were going to just go straight from work but if we're going out out I wanted to get changed, have a shower, do my make-up. I've got a good feeling about tonight so I want to look my best. Smell my best. Dare I say, taste my best? Would I be that fortunate? If Stevie is out that would be a certainty. If Stevie knows I'm out then him being out would be a certainty. Ergo, I'm getting bare laid tonight, fam. Amber's looking very good too, I've got to say. She's always scrubbed up really well. She doesn't tart it up or anything. She's got class. To me she's got the look of a sexy cat. I know, I know, how can cats be sexy? You know what I mean though, she's got these big eyes and a small nose. Cat-like. And I don't mind saying that she's sexy. Like I say, she's got class. I pour her a glass of fizz and stick some tunes on. My mum and dad are through in the living room watching telly, so it's on quiet. I don't take the piss.
"How mad was that about Big Barry at work?" I say. It's been scratching away at me all day since it happened. Amber laughs.
"Ohmagod, I know, Sprinkle's got bare problems," she says. I frown.
"Don't be like that," I say, "what if he'd died?"
Her face straightens up and she mutters sorry. She quickly takes a mouthful of fizz.
"You don't need to be sorry. I just don't think he needs people laughing about it. He's obviously got problems,

and I'm sure having to work in that place doesn't help. Did you see Tara made him go back online? Not enough availability for him to go and get himself checked out. That's bare harsh that."
"Ohmagod, did she? What a bitch."
I nod, and empty my glass. It's almost half eight. The taxi should be here soon so the music goes off and we move through to the living room. My mum and dad are watching some stand-up comedian on telly that they put on pause.
"Is that you out then?" Dad asks.
"Taxi's due at half eight," I say.
"You look nice," he says, then spends too long looking at Amber's legs and tits. My mum definitely notices.
"Thanks," I say, "I might be staying at hers tonight, but will you leave the door off the latch in case I don't, please?"
Mum's in a mood now because Dad got busted getting an eyeful of his daughter's friend, but she mumbles yes as her hand reaches for the remote and presses play. The northern comedian tells a joke and the crowd laugh, and my dad laughs, but nobody else laughs.

In the taxi, I'm still thinking about Barry from work. The taxi driver is banging on about nothing, his wild eyes in the rear view mirror flick from me to Amber to me to Amber as he chats shit. Amber's talking to him but I can't be arsed. What's got Barry to the point that he wants to off himself, at work too? If it were me, and it won't ever be me, I'd do it privately. But it's never going to be nice, is it? A stranger finding you or your dad finding you, it's gonna fuck somebody up for life. I don't know, I can't get my head round it. You've got to be in a dark place. I do a loud sigh. One of those ones you can't control. One you barely even realise you've done. Amber asks me if I'm alright. I say yes, but Barry's still baking my head. Stevie takes the piss out of him a fair bit, but it's just bantz is all. He doesn't mean anything by it. There's something messing him up. I pull my phone out and find him on Facebook. He's got no mutual friends, and only about fifty friends at all, which is sad in itself. His profile picture is a cartoon wizard. His photos are just a lot of those shitty inspirational quotes typed over a sunset. There are a few selfies of him taken from his webcam, but not much else.

"Who are you stalking?" Amber says leaning across to me, but I just shake my head and say nobody. His statuses don't give much away. He's got zero likes on any of them. I'm wondering if he's just really lonely. Like, he finds it hard to make friends? I make a decision to keep my eye on him. Like, not get too close, he might be a bare freak, but if I just say hi and ask him if he's okay now and then. He might appreciate that. It'll be good karma too, and we all know what a bitch karma can be.

"Just here please," says Amber as the taxi moves to the kerb and stops by the eighties bar. They do nice cocktails there, even if the music is rubbish, and it's cheap. It's always a good starting point. After this it'll be the Wetherspoons, then Yates's. It never gets super busy in town on a Thursday, so we can just do our thing and not get pestered by wankers or bitches. I don't like clubs in town. They're populated by rapey Eastern Europeans and skanks. We'll always go to one of the good the city if we're planning on doing a bit of raving, but those nights aren't that common to be honest. I'd rather save the cash and go to a house party. Danny from work rents his own place so we tend to get bare smashed at his, every now and then. He's got a back garden so it's all about the barbecues in Summer too. You can always make sure you're playing the tunes you like, doing the drugs you like, and hanging out with people you like. Win win, as they say. Anyway, we get into the eighties bar and it's dead. There's two older women in the corner, watching the door like hawks, waiting for some unsuspecting lads so they can pounce and give out some of that cougar action. You can tell this is the case because they go all deflated and annoyed when we walk through the door all glammed up. We get our drinks and move to a booth down the back. Amber's gone for a Mojito and I'm on the Pina Colada. Classics, you could say. We chat about boys, and work, and Amber's telling me she's applied for the college course she's mentioned to me a few times. It's a leisure and tourism qualification she's talking about. She wants to work on the cruise ships, see some of the world. Her big eyes light up when she tells me too. Bless her, I'm happy for her. It'll give her a better chance of getting out of that fucking call centre. I need to do something with my own life myself. I promised myself it was just a stop gap to earn some money so I could go travelling, and it's coming up to a year I've been there. You want to know how much I've saved so far? Nothing. I know I'm only young and there's still time but there are people that have worked there twenty years who are still earning the same as me. How is that even legal?

Verbal Warning

People doing a job longer than I've been alive, still earning just over minimum wage? I'm not getting into it just now though. There's plenty of time to meet the infected yet.

"I start in September," says Amber with a happy smile, "you should look into it too."

"Oh, can you imagine the trouble we'd get into on the ships together?" I laugh. The truth is that I won't be doing it. I want to see the world on my own terms, not serving drinks and seeing the world through a window. I know, I know. There's more to it than that, but you know what I mean. I want to do a Full Moon Party in Koh Phangan, and work in a bar to earn my digs in Melbourne. I want to sit on a beach in South Africa watching the sun set. I want to do travelling, properly. Like I see everybody doing on Instagram. I want my Instagram to have more than just us in a shitty eighties bar in town. That said, I do love a filtered double selfie so I've got my phone out and Amber and I push our heads together, straws coming out of our cocktails into our mouths. We smile big daft smiles and I take the photo. I flick through the filters, blur it up and stick a border on it, then upload it. Hashtag selfie. Hashtag bezzies. Hashtag cocktails. Hashtag everything. I get seven likes straight away from a load of randomers, then one from Stevie.

About half an hour later he comes steaming into the bar with a bloke I recognise from the sales team. Callum, I think. He's shagged one of my other mates. She says he was shit. I almost feel bad for Amber. Almost. The older women perk up as the boys come in, then deflate again as Stevie slides into the booth next to me, and Callum next to Amber.

"Alright, Penny?" Stevie says, his smooth tanned face looking very dark and his teeth looking very white in the blue light of the bar.

"Hi, Stevie."

From there, the boys go on a full on charm offensive, giving it bare large. I smile in all the right places, but I'm not listening. I'm looking at the twinkle in Stevie's eyes, watching the way his lips crunch together after he takes a drink. When he and Callum go to the toilet I watch his arse. He's a very fine specimen, it has to be said. Amber asks if we can go, I shake my head and give her the puppy dogs. She tells me that Callum has put his hand on her leg four times and his breath stinks rotten. Like farts, she says. I don't want her to have a shitty night for my benefit, sisters before misters, as they say. So I nod and we drink our drinks and slide out of the booth. We're almost at the door when Stevie's voice calls out. He looks hurt that we were leaving, and his hurt face is even sexier than his normal face. I ask for his phone, and when he gives it to me I tap in my number. I tell him to text me in a couple of hours. I tell him to get rid of his mate by then. He smiles and nods, wide eyed. There's cocaine around his nostrils. I go up on tip toes and into his ear I tell him to wipe his nose. He does.

Exactly two hours later the text comes. Exactly thirty minutes after that we're kissing in a taxi to Stevie's. Exactly thirty minutes after that, well, I'm sure you can guess. Just because I know how to take the emotion out of sex it doesn't mean I'm crass enough to tell you every minute detail of my private life. We fall asleep, and I wake at about five in the morning. Stevie

Verbal Warning

is snoring loudly, so I grab my things and head home. I'm back in my own bed by six, and I'm asleep until midday.

After Call Work

FRIDAY

Verbal Warning

Chapter Five

Barry

I wake up at half past seven and switch on my main computer. I need to check if the Epic Sword I had on at the auction has sold. It dropped in Upper Blackrock Spire. That probably doesn't make sense to you, I'm sorry. I should explain. On my days off I play World of Warcraft. It's a really good online role playing game. My main character is a Priest, which means I get to do healing when we do dungeon raids. The good thing about healers is that everybody needs them. There are so many people who want to be attackers and cause damage that sometimes there aren't enough people to heal them in battle. Everybody needs a healer. My character name is BlessedBarry, which I think is clever in a few ways. First, there's the two Bs in it, so it rolls off the tongue. Second, my character is a Priest, and he's blessed. Do you get it? Clever, eh? Anyway, on the game I'm in a guild, which is basically a gang. I'm the Guild master, so I decide who gets to join. There are fifteen people in my guild so far. There are six members of a family from South Africa who all play together, and the rest are from England. I've never met any of them yet, but they're the closest thing to best friends that I have. There are even girls in my guild. The Warlock called VoraciousVixen. That's a girl called Sally. I look at her Facebook a lot. She's pretty. Sometimes we don't even do dungeon raids. Sometimes we just have duels and talk about our days. Usually, I can tell them anything, that's how close we are. Usually. What happened yesterday though, I can't

After Call Work

tell them. I'm the Guild master. I'm supposed to be the leader. To them I'm the main healer. What happens when the healer needs healing, though? I can't do it. As the WoW load bar shifts across the screen and the world appears before me I shut it down. The sword can wait. I can't face my guild. Not yet. Instead, I load up my browser and go to Facebook. There are no notifications, as usual. From my search history I bring up Jake Kilner. He hasn't said anything about what I did. I go to check Twitter and again there's nothing. Obviously some of it is going to take time, but he should have at least received a lot of spam email, surely? If he has then he doesn't care, clearly. Very annoying. I pull up a list of takeaways near his house from online and save the telephone numbers. For later, of course. It's far too early for any of that. Or is it? I filter the search engine to bring up only those outlets that sell breakfasts and such. There are five where his house is within their delivery areas. It's a start. Taking care to withhold my number I order twenty pounds' worth of food from each. Nothing silly, just enough to upset him. I give his home telephone number as the contact to all of them and go back to the social media websites, refreshing them every few seconds. It takes five minutes before it happens. NICE TRY WHOEVER ORDERD FOOD 2 MY HOUSE. THEY CALLED TO CHECK AND I CANCLD IT. HAHAHAHAHA. Annoying. But not the end of the world. A handful of comments of people querying what had happened appear, and Jake Kilner responds telling them the story of how he foiled a prank plan. A dozen people are tagged as potential culprits, and over the next few minutes they each deny involvement. Before long

Verbal Warning

there it is. WHAT THE FUCK? I DONT EVEN LYK BROWN SAUCE!!!!!!!!!!! and a picture of five breakfast sandwiches on what looks to be his kitchen table. He tells the story to his friends. He paid for the delivery. He was starving and wasn't going to be beaten by one of his dickhead mates. He was gutted about the brown sauce, because brown sauce is for wankers. Now he's twenty quid out of pocket. When he finds out who did it they owe him. Two more minutes pass until SRSLY PISSED OF NOW!!!! 3 MORE DELVRYS SHOWD UP. WITCH PRICK IS MUGGIN ME OF?? ILL KICK UR ASS!!!!

Jake Kilner's stress entertains me for the full morning, which passes very quickly. I've scratched the five food outlets from my list of around thirty in his area. They won't fall for it again. The rest can wait until this evening. At around one in the afternoon I get a notification. A friend request. My stomach flips and turns. I half expect it to be from Jake Kilner, as if the Facebook police have seen that I've spent all morning watching his troubles and let him know. They haven't. My stomach flips and turns even more when the request is from Penny Clarke. The girl at work who defended me. Stevie's friend. Why would she friend request me? Is he behind it? Both of them laughing at me. Looking to harass me at home as well as work? They can stick that right up their bums. But she defended me. I don't get it. What would she possibly want with me? She obviously doesn't fancy me. I mean, come on, look at me. Look at her. Look at her. I do. I click onto her profile and her photos. She's so beautiful. There are pictures of her in a bikini on her

After Call Work

holiday, her on a beach towel on her hands and knees and she's got her bum sticking out and looking at the camera and. No. I turn her profile off and go back to Jake Kilner. His final thread about the food deliveries has almost fifty comments. Some of them express a suspicion that he's lying and that he's just a fat bastard who wanted five sandwiches. Others continue to suggest potential candidates. Others. Others. Penny Clarke. Did she friend request me by accident? Why was she looking at me in the first place? I don't get it. That holiday picture though. I go back to it. I right click it and I save it but I'm already ashamed. I'm back at Jake Kilner. I'm back at Penny Clarke. I avoid her photos and look at her profile. Stevie has liked everything she has put on there. Pictures of her in town with that girl Amber who calls me Sprinkle. She's never said why she calls me that, but I know it's done in a mean way because there's a look in her eyes. I don't like her. I don't like anybody that Penny hangs around with, and I hardly know Penny. She's spoken to me twice, and one of those times was yesterday. She has kind eyes, but her friends. My hand moves the cursor over the button to reject her request. She's just like her friends, I know it. But then why the heck has she requested me? I don't know that I'm strong enough to deal with what she has for me. Whatever cruelty she has up her sleeve. I can be though. I can be. I click back to Jake Kilner and I move through his photo albums. I save lots of them. I find his girlfriend. She's very pretty. I search for her on all of the social media sites until I find her email address. She has a blog where she talks about music. It's very popular. She likes bands like Arctic Monkeys and Foo Fighters.

Verbal Warning

She shares her experiences of concerts she goes to. She seems nice. Too nice for Jake blumming Kilner. I find lots of dating websites and I sign Jake Kilner up for profiles. I sign him up for lots of profiles. My version of Jake Kilner likes men. He likes women. My version of him likes to dress up as a lady. He likes to take sex drugs and go to sex parties. My version of Jake Kilner won't say no to anything. Then I use his girlfriend's email address to register him to the sites. I use the pictures I stole from his Facebook, and then I go back to his profile, and I wait to see what he says. There's nothing for a while, just more and more comments about his experience with the sandwich deliveries. Then nothing. Jake Kilner stops responding. I go to look at his girlfriend's profile. It's there. Her single word status. Heartbroken. A sad emoji face with a tear in its eye. Then the questions. What's up hun? Why? What's happened? OMG what? Her response? I'll inbox you. Jake Kilner adds his own status within seconds. SOME1 IS MESSIN WIT DA WRONG MAN. FIRST THE DELIVRYS AN NOW YOU TRYIN 2 FUK UP MY RELATIONSHIP? I FIND OUT WHOSE DOIN IT UR A DEAD MAN. GET A LYF. I believe he means it, too.

After Call Work

Chapter Six

Penny

When I go downstairs after showering there's nobody in. Mum and dad will both be at work. In the lounge, a duvet is folded up on the end of the sofa. They've obviously had a fight after Amber and I went out, and Dad has lost. They'll be fine. There isn't a month goes by when mum doesn't get at least one night in their bed to herself. I swear she sometimes picks arguments just so she can have a night starfished on her own. She's always been feisty, my mum. She used to do kickboxing when she was younger. It's how she got together with my dad. He used to be dead fat, and really fancied her but she smashed him straight into the friend zone. He started going to the same gym as her, and got bare hench. I don't mind saying, my dad was a stunner when he was younger. I'm proud of him. Anyway, eventually she saw what he was doing. He was working so hard to put himself in her league. He was doing it for her. He asked her out and the rest is history. The thing is, my dad is always going to be that fat kid at heart, so my mum is always going to be the boss. Ergo, my dad puts a foot out of line and he gets a night on the sofa.

I make myself some toast while I tinker about on my phone. Stevie hasn't text. Of course he hasn't. This is Stevie we're talking about. He's had his fun, I dare say he'll probably avoid me at work for a few days too. Making sure he puts distance between us so I don't fall in love. As if. You're a fine looking man and a generous

Verbal Warning

lover, Steven Weller, but a long term prospect you most certainly are not. Plus, he is pretty stupid. He's got the gift of the gab, but he can't spell. He can charm your pants off but he couldn't tell you where Reykjavik was. You get what I'm saying, I'm sure. I won't milk it. I go on to check my Facebook and it goes straight onto Big Barry from work's profile since I haven't been on since the taxi last night. Big depressed Barry. The tragic bastard. I look at the memes he's shared. The generic sunset. The phrases. Pulling others down won't help you to reach the top. People talking behind your back are where they belong, behind you. What the fuck, though? There's a definite meme theme here. Where does he find this shit? How does he think it's going to help him? They look like the anti-bullying posters from the counsellor's office from school. I don't think he's being bullied though. He strikes me as the sensitive type, probably even oversensitive. Maybe takes things a little too much to heart. Bless him. I really think he just needs somebody to talk to. I mean take these pictures he's parading to his fifty Facebook friends. They're cries for somebody to ask him what's up. That's what they are. That's not even the most tragic part. The most tragic part is that literally nobody is paying them any attention at all. He's crying into a vacuum of pure ignorance. Now I've seen it, I feel this overwhelming sense of duty, you know? If he goes and actually succeeds in offing himself, I'm going to feel bare guilty. It might only take the smallest thing. Fuck's sake. Me and my massive conscience. I click to friend request him without a second thought. It's not much, but it's me reaching out. I'm still not going to his house for dinner, but I

After Call Work

hope he appreciates that somebody has acknowledged his pain in some way. I move to my own profile and upload the Instagram picture of Amber and I with our cocktails and make it my profile picture. We look pretty fit, it has to be said. We. Right. Look, I'm not being gross here, but if you're here for a while I'm not going to be able to hide it from you for long. Please don't think bad of me, but my fanny is proper itching. Even after my shower I'm scratching at it like anything. It's not comfortable at all. My first thought is that I've maybe left a bit of shower creme down there. You know? Not rinsed right? But I was very thorough. I always am after, well, you know. My second thought is an STI, but Stevie and I were careful, so I'm certain it's not the clap or anything. I mean, Stevie's a lad I would never in a million years let near me without protection, I hope you believe me. He's probably riddled with chlamydia. I know, I know. But if you'd seen him in real life you'd understand why I had to, you know, with him. My third thought, and the one that sticks with me the longest, is that he's given me fucking crabs. I Google the symptoms of pubic lice as I climb the stairs to the bathroom two at a time and whip down my pyjama bottoms. The symptoms are:

* Itching in the affected areas - Yes. There's fucking itching.
* Black powdery droppings from the lice in your underwear - Not yet, but lice shit in my knickers? Fucking lice shit in my fucking knickers?
* Brown eggs on pubic or other body hair - I don't know. There's not much hair but what there is, is dark. I can't tell.

Verbal Warning

* Irritation and inflammation in the affected area, sometimes caused by scratching - Yes. I've been scratching.
* Sky-blue spots (which disappear within a few days) or very tiny specks of blood on the skin - Yes. There are.

He's given me crabs. The absolute wanker. I grab my phone and dial the bastard's number. He doesn't answer for the first five times I ring, but I'm not going away so he finally relents on the sixth.
"Penny, babe, what's up? Last night was-"
"You prick."
"What? What's up?"
"You've passed some of your little friends on."
"What are you talking about?"
"Crabs. Stevie. You've given me crabs, you scummy bastard."
He goes quiet, and then I hear him laughing. It's not any kind of shocked nervous laughter either, he actually thinks it's funny. I can't get my breath.
"Now that you mention it, I've been itching this morning too," he laughs, "I wasn't before. How do you know it's not you that's passed them to me?"
"Because, Stevie, I left the house last night with no crabs on my fanny. I spend a few hours with you and now suddenly there are crabs on my fanny. The last time I had a shag was-" I pause, it's none of his business. "It doesn't matter when. The fact is you've passed your grubby little mates on to me and I am pissed right off."
He doesn't say anything for a few, maybe even ten seconds. Then when he does he blows my mind.

After Call Work

"So, what do you want me to do about it? I'm happy to come and lick them off. If you want?"

I scream down the phone as he laughs, and I hang up. I scream again in frustration. I don't know what I expected of that phone call. An apology would have been a good start. An acknowledgement. Anything other than amused indifference and piss taking. What the hell am I supposed to do now? Help me out here. Have you ever had crabs? Do I have to go to the doctor or what? I know, I know. You're only here as a spectator to this drama called my life. It's a one way street. With a sigh, I'm back and searching online. It looks like I've got lucky, if lucky could ever be the right word. It's a trip to the chemist next on the agenda, then back here to clear up the problem. The biggest annoyance, after the itching, is that it could be a week before it's actually cleared up. Seriously, I could fucking kill Stevie. First, I've got to kill these little things he's so generously shared with me. When I called him a generous lover this wasn't quite what I meant. God, this itching is infuriating. It's totally killed my long weekend. Look, no offence to you or anything, but I'd rather be on my own for a while. I've got this to sort out, so I'll see you in a bit, yeah?

Verbal Warning

SUNDAY

After Call Work

Chapter Seven

Barry

Things have developed with Jake Kilner. He and his girlfriend are back together. She believes that he didn't sign up for dating profiles. Whoever did it didn't take into account that he was massively homophobic, and a lover of men was the last thing that Jake Kilner would ever be. He's still upset, though, about the eight different pizza deliveries that arrived at his door last night. It's consuming him, this not knowing who is messing with him. He's threatened the police, violence, and financial rewards for anybody that will grass on whoever is doing it. He'll never catch on that it's me, though. He'll never remember the jobsworth virgin that he was so rude to on the telephone. I was just another faceless voice for him to deal with and then forget all about. That power he thought he had as the customer, like he could do and say anything he wanted to me because it was my job to take it. Well guess what, Jake Kilner? You picked on the wrong man at the wrong time. Now it's my turn to upset you, and doing so is really addictive. I still don't know if my Epic Sword sold at auction. I don't know if my guild miss me. This is the longest time I have gone away from them since forever, and I have Jake Kilner to thank for it. In three days I have gone from a level one mischief maker to a level twenty mischief maker. Anonymity is my armour, the Internet is my weapon. This game is uncapped though, there is no limit to what I can do to make his life a misery. Dating profiles and unexpected pizza deliveries are just quests I need

Verbal Warning

to complete to gain experience. I'm sorry, Jake Kilner, but I'm not sorry. We have a long way to go together yet. You're my own personal secret punching bag. I'm so many other people's. Why shouldn't I have one of my own?

The red blob still sits next to the friend request icon on my Facebook page. An unanswered notification. Penny Clarke. I daren't accept or decline her request. I don't have anybody on there from work. Why would I? They treat me like crap. All of them. Why would I want them in my personal life? But Penny. She's so blumming beautiful. What if it's genuine and she wants me, I mean, wants to know me? What if she is different to the others? I get butterflies when I think of her now, and I don't know her at all. Before Thursday she was nothing to me; a loud mouthed pretty girl that was friends with him. But then she defended me and friended me. Then there was that picture of her in Tenerife. Then. Now. Now she has a name. Now she's Penny Clarke. I should wait until tomorrow at work. I should see if she speaks with me, and if she does I will see how she speaks with me. Then I will know if she's actually my friend.

After Call Work

Chapter Eight

Penny

There's some Victorian type crap on the telly tonight, and mum watches it in silence as my dad makes dinner. I flick from Facebook to Instagram to Snapchat to Instagram again without really focusing on anything. The picture of Amber and I has three hundred or so likes. Not bad. Barry from work still hasn't accepted my request, so there's the added guilt that he could be dead and dangling from the big light in his bedroom, on top of me being two days into a week long course of treatment for pubic lice. Yeah, I went to the chemist. You can buy it over the counter but not before a lecture from the old Asian woman about sexual health and do I want advice about seeking tests for other sexually transmitted diseases? Do I need counselling and other such? Have I told my other recent sexual partners? Mate, it was bare humiliating. But I got through it and here I am. I try to take my mind off Barry and the crabs with a game of Candy Crush but it's no good. I'm stuck on one of the hard levels where you die after three moves if you don't get it right first time, so my lives are all gone within five minutes and I'm back to checking Facebook and Snapchat and Instagram for updates that aren't there. Stevie hasn't been in touch either, which is as irritating as the crabs he gave to me. I don't want anything to do with him, to be honest, but just a text to see if I'm alright or to see what I've done about the lice, would mark him out as less of an utter prick than he actually is.

Verbal Warning

"Dinner will be five minutes, ladies," my dad shouts from the kitchen. My mum fires some evil death stares at the door and turns back to the telly. My dad's obviously still on her shit list, which is weird. I mean, yeah, he got busted looking at an eighteen year old girl's tits in his own living room, but Amber is gorgeous. Even I'd fuck her. I think my mum's being a bit harsh, but what do I know? My dad's making some Italian chicken stuff with pasta. He's a good cook, to be fair. He finds recipes that he likes the look of and then bangs about a hundred other ingredients in to make them different but in a good way. The only time he has really fucked it up was when he made us a casserole with beer in, but forgot to add anything but beer. Like, no water or anything. It was an awful sticky mess that tasted like shit. We ended up ordering a curry that night and my dad never did casserole again.

At the dinner table it's weird. I don't make much conversation because of the shit that's swirling around my head. My mum takes tiny bites of her food and nudges what's on her plate with her fork, like she's searching for bits she can stomach. My dad happily eats his way through his. He's on dangerous ground with that, though, because my mum's bare ready to explode. My dad looks at me with a frown. "You okay, Pen? You're quiet," he says. I nod and smile a thin smile as I tell him I'm fine. I'm just tired. He smiles too and carries on eating. He really doesn't understand women, bless him, but he knows enough to know that *I'm fine, I'm just tired* is code for *Don't ask*. My mum sighs, and dad just looks at her and then back to his dinner. He also knows a powder keg when he sees one. There's no chance of him lighting the fuse if he can help it.

Verbal Warning

MONDAY

After Call Work

Chapter Nine

Barry

I swipe through the security gate and back into the belly of the building. It's quiet at this time of day, as there are only a handful of contracts that have eight o'clock starts, and the way my buses run means I have to get here at seven fifteen or I get here late. You're only allowed three lates or you get taken to disciplinary, and then you've spoiled your chances at any kind of a promotion for nine months. It's unfair, but I suppose they're the experts in knowing what makes us better at our jobs. They're the experts in making us better people. It's even there as the slogan across the wall of the balcony that hangs over reception. *TeleWeb. Experts in people.* If it's in writing, it must be true, eh?

The canteen is closed this early, so I go to my desk and load up my computer. The Oriental girl who does the early morning cleaning is taking her time to dust the keyboards and telephones. She dusts around everything, rather than under and on. I've spoken with HR about it, but they say it's up to facilities to deal with. I've spoken to facilities, who say they're an external contractor. I couldn't find the contact details of the external contractor, so I spend my time sighing at her when she cleans around me and my work station. She doesn't pay any attention to it. Why would she? Nobody else does.

Verbal Warning

People begin to show up and start to load their own computers up at about half past seven, and conversations begin about what happened over people's weekends. I overhear somebody tell somebody else about the amount of drugs they took. Somebody else says their football team lost, but promotion is still a possibility. The person they are talking to doubts that very much. Somebody else won big at the casino. They play poker. They made it to the next round of a competition. They're happy about that. Seven forty five comes round and more people are here. Darren, my manager, is here and at his computer. Somebody asks for five minutes of his time and he tells them to wait until eight o'clock. He's checking his emails and booking rooms. The client is on site today and as the early shift manager it's up to him to ensure everything is prepared. *The client visit.* The time of the week when everybody has to act professional. Cups and food are strictly prohibited. Wrap has to be kept to a minimum. Talking to anybody but your customer or your manager is not permitted. Anybody not wearing business dress will be sent home and must return within an hour in suitable attire. It's all a load of blumming rubbish. We all have to pretend like this is how it's run all of the time. It's the same when we have an audit. Managers all running around like headless chickens, and filling out paperwork that says we've all had our weekly coaching sessions. I've tried to tell HR about it, but they don't listen. Did you expect anything else?

At seven fifty eight, *he* comes strolling in. Steven. He logs his telephone to show that he's on site, but then

he moves across to Dave from Jim's team to have a chat. His computer stays turned off. Dave is scary. He is covered in tattoos, from his fingers up to his face, and then probably everywhere that I wouldn't wish to imagine. He listens to rap music, but he's *white*. He draws mushrooms on everything. He's weird. The pair of them talk until after eight o'clock and Darren has shouted at everybody to get online. I haven't pressed to go into ready yet, as I'm watching Dave and Steven talking and laughing. Does anybody else not see what they are doing? Then they both stop talking and look off behind me. I turn to see her. Penny. She doesn't look happy. Dave and Steven laugh, and make their fists his each other. Steven scratches at his crotch and laughs. He points at Penny. She shakes her head and walks to the coat rail. She doesn't look my way even once. Dave and Steven hit their hands together again.
"Barry, can I have you in ready?" Darren calls to me. I don't say anything but I make a point of looking at Steven and then back to Darren, "did you hear me, mate? Get in ready."
It's like Steven is completely invisible and immune to any form of telling off. If this isn't favouritism then I don't know what is. Penny walks past him and he nods his head with a smile and says hi to her. She doesn't respond. She just goes to her team and sits down, putting her headset on and apologising to Jim, her manager. I watch her for a few seconds. She's so beautiful, so effortlessly beautiful, that it hurts. My stomach rolls and-
"Barry! What are you doing?" Darren is standing up, hands on his hips, and looking right at me. "We've got the client on site today, don't give me any shit, okay?"

Verbal Warning

And there we go. The concern and the best friend act he was playing last week has gone. I'm back to being his most hated employee, and Steven. Lucky, awful Steven is allowed to walk in when he feels like it and do anything he blumming well wants to. Again, I just look to my bully, and I say nothing. I press to go into ready to take a call, and one immediately comes through.

It's eighty thirty six exactly when Steven is actually taking calls. He spent his time wandering the length of the call floor, stopping to talk to boys and girls. When he talked to boys he nodded towards Penny and laughed, and when he talked to girls his eyes went all narrow and his stance changed. Trying to get into their pants, no doubt. I look at Penny, and she doesn't seem her usual self. As if I know what her usual self is. She's staring at her computer and talking to customers. Some people who come in ready for the nine o'clock shift wave at her but she just smiles and carries on. Something has happened this weekend just gone, and if I had anything to do with gambling, I would bet all of the gold that my Epic Sword might have made at auction that it was something to do with Steven. I wish I'd accepted her friend request now. Maybe she knows what he's like and wanted somebody to talk to. But I didn't, and now she's just a girl with a lot on her mind. I've let her down. But I won't again. I can promise you that. I'll take her under my wing and I'll protect her.
"Psst, Fat Fuck," says Steven, "you don't want her, she's damaged goods."

After Call Work

My focus hits Steven, and he's looking at me with a grin.
"What?" I ask.
"Penny, you've been staring at her all morning like she's made of tits."
His hand comes up, and a finger extends.
"One, she's so far out of your chubby Diabetes Type Two league. Seriously, you're blind football with the little bell inside the ball, and she's fucking Barcelona, mate. You think a piece of arse like that would let a fat cunt like you even smell her chair?"
A second finger goes up.
"Two, she's riddled with crabs. Abso-fucking-letely riddled with them. I fucked her this weekend, she's passed them on to me. Can you believe it? She's given me crabs. Got to see a doctor at some point and get them cleaned up."
"Crabs?" I say. I don't understand. Steven laughs.
"Crabs, nits in her pubs, mate. She's got lice on her fanny."
He's lying. I tell him as much and he laughs again.
"She's not the angel you think she is. She's hungry for cock, mate, but she'd have to be starving to the level of getting Comic Relief donations to have a go on yours."
"I don't know what you're talking about," I say.
Then he shouts her name, and she looks up. He makes a circle with one hand and then pokes a finger into it. She raises her middle finger to him and turns back to her computer screen.
"Barry. Seriously. Get some fucking calls taken."
I turn to see Darren, once again, staring at me like I've committed a murder. Steven laughs again, and I take another call. As my customer passes DPA Steven holds

Verbal Warning

up his whiteboard. On it, it says *while theirs stray dogs on the street an sheeps in feelds your shit out of luck fat cunt.*

After Call Work

Chapter Ten

Penny

What a prick. I know, I know. What did I expect? I don't care that anybody knows that I've shagged him. I'd openly admit that. You should hopefully know me by now to know I'm quite an honest person, I'll say it like it is and if you don't like me for it then you can go and fuck yourself. But to go and start telling people it was *me* that passed them onto *him*? Unforgivable. He's not going to get away with it, I can tell you that much. Between calls, I've been putting an email together. I'll let you see it when it's done, I'm not giving you a bit then talking some more and then giving you a bit more. For the most part, it's probably going to confuse you. I'm not saying you're thick, far from it, I mean, you're here in the first place so unless you stumbled in looking for something else. I dunno, something *wizardy* then you've probably got enough upstairs to get what's happening, but I'm just talking about the new people. You've always got to go to your slowest learner, haven't you? Anyway, there's a client on site so Jim's been flapping for the first couple of hours. He's had Tony off the phones and floor walking while he makes sure everything's ready for Sam and Andy. They're from the client. They're not that special, I mean, they're here every week. They aren't anything higher than the managers we have here at their own office, but they're, say it quietly, *the client*. Basically they just come and look around and make sure we're still behaving ourselves while we're doing the job for them. They're the very top of the hierarchy. It goes:

Verbal Warning

* Us, the shit on the shoes of the world - here to take as much crap as the customers can give, as much crap as the managers can give, as much crap as the health and safety people want to give, as much crap as the compliance people want to give. We're shit, basically. We have jobs here because we need these jobs more than these jobs need us. These jobs are easy to get. They can always fill our chairs with equally stupid arses if we don't like it. They've said as much themselves.

* The managers – little Hitler pricks who were either in the right place at the right time, or managed to slide their slimy tongues into the right arses at the right time. Being a manager consists mainly of shouting at the *world to get out of wrap* and pretending to the Operations Managers like they know what they're doing. They don't. They basically live by the phrase, *I don't have to know how to do your job, I just have to know how to tell you to do it.*

* The Operations Managers. AKA Ops – sit by their computers answering emails all day, calling the managers into pointless meetings about why they aren't doing their jobs, then not actually doing anything to help the managers do their jobs. They get paid less than you'd think, but the money's not the reason why they do it. The reason is that they can actually smell the position above them, where they don't have to deal with the peasants anymore. It's like the limbo of middle management. In the real world,

After Call Work

though, having Operations Manager on your CV is as valuable as having *Unicorn Shit Shoveller* on there.

* The whatever the hell your job is – the dickhead who shows up once in a blue moon. You never know what their actual job title is, but you know they're the boss. When they show up it's much the same as when the client shows up. Like the Queen just stopped by to watch us all answering calls from angry customers we couldn't give two fucks about.

* The Client – the one who, ultimately, pays our wages. Although, they pay TeleWeb about twice what TeleWeb pay us. I know this because I've been to their head office for a visit once. It was to see what went on there. Like, some sort of team building thing. I had to stay overnight, and I might have shagged one of their managers. He might have told me. I'm not saying I did, but I might have. Okay, I did. It was alright. Nothing to sing from the rooftops about. Anyway. Whoever they send, whether it's the director, or the manager, or the man who serves them sandwiches at dinner time, the client is boss. You don't talk to the client unless the client talks to you first. You don't speak ill of the client. You don't cross the client.

Shit, isn't it?

So the dreaded client isn't even here yet, but it's not stopped Tony strutting around like he owns the place. I mean, floor walking is shit. I've done it once, and all you get is a hundred hands pointed in the air wanting some sort of help. No thanks. Fuck that. It's not my

Verbal Warning

scene. I'll just do the job I'm paid to do, thank you very much. But for those who have aspirations of making it as high as manager level, floor walking is the Holy Grail. A chance to show how good at your job you are. When Ops are out and about, you can often find the Lesser Spotted Floorwalker hovering about, looking for somebody to help. I once heard Tony, and I swear I'm not making this up, he was talking to somebody about nothing, and he spotted Patrick walking up from being outside having a cigarette. "Oh, Patrick's coming, I need to go and find somebody to help over there so he sees me," he said. I could have turned myself inside out I cringed with that much embarrassment. I mean, come on, get a grip of your life.

I haven't just been talking to you here in wrap or personal time, by the way. My customer has me on hold so he can go and find his bank card. I can't let you hear his card number when he comes back. I'll have to pause the recording. That's the rules. There are a lot of rules here. More rules than seven pounds an hour should dictate, to be fair, but I refer to my previous point about somebody filling your chair if you don't like it.
"Hey, baby."
A friendly voice. Amber. I smile up at her and put my call on mute.
"Hiya, how are you?" I say with a thin smile.
"I'm okay. What about you? I heard what Stevie's saying. It's not true, is it?"
I unmute my customer, who has come back.

After Call Work

"Thank you, please bear with me whilst I pause the recording to be able to take your details," I say to the customer, and mute the call.
"What? That I gave him crabs?" I say to Amber. She nods. I scrunch up my face. "No, it's not. It's the other way around."
"Now if you can give me the long number from the front of the card?" I say to the customer, who does.
"So you slept with him then?" Amber says. I nod.
"And the expiry date please?"
"And he gave you crabs?" Amber says. I nod.
"And the last three digits on the back of the card, please."
"Dirty bastard," Amber says. I nod.
"Thank you, please bear with me whilst the payment processes. It may take a few seconds." I place the customer on mute.
"Now he's going round saying it was me that gave them to him," I say to Amber. She frowns.
"Thank you, that payment has been processed, your payment reference number will be texted to you shortly, thank you for calling today."
I put myself into wrap- AKA after call work –and turn to Amber.
"I know, and he's pissed me off. I'm bare pissed off, Am. Seriously. Bare. Pissed. Off."

Verbal Warning

Chapter Eleven

Barry

There's a TeleWeb meeting scheduled in for two o'clock this afternoon. It's only just showed up on the scheduler now. It's for half an hour. I look to Darren to ask what it's for but he's up busy, walking around with what looks like purpose. I haven't seen him this active since the last time the client were on site. I've heard him say that Martin Rose is on site too though, which is double bad for those of us on the phones. Except Steven though, obviously. This means even more intense scrutiny with everything that we do. Martin Rose is Patrick's boss. I'm not sure exactly what his job is, but he is in charge of our contract and some others in different offices. All I know, other than that, is that he makes jobs up for people. People that he likes. He just makes positions up and puts people into them. For example, I heard Tony from Jim's team complaining that a man that used to work here was taken off the phones to look after a contract on another site for a few months. When Martin told him to come back and work on the phones again, he started crying. Nothing wrong with that, of course, I cry. But because he'd started crying, Martin suddenly had the position of Client Liaison Account Coordinator available and the man now works in another office on twice as much money as us. I heard that there is now a senior version of that job being filled by another person, and two assistants. Do you think it's worth going to speak to HR about? No. Me neither.
"Daz, what's this meeting at two all about?" Steven

After Call Work

calls out as Darren races past. I have a call going on in my ear so I don't get a lot of the response. Something about meetings and news. Steven shouts something about getting a pay rise but Darren shakes his head as he strides off and away from us. Steven looks at me and sticks his middle finger up.
"They're sacking all the fat bastards," he says quietly, "did you buy some stronger laces?"
I say nothing, but somewhere in the back of my mind, I can hear the groan of Jake Kilner as another pornographic DVD sample pack is delivered to his door.
"I'm surprised you came back, to be fair," says Steven, "if it were me that tried and failed to take the coward's way out, I'd be dead of shame."
Somewhere in the back of my mind, Jake Kilner is annoyed that the British Heart Foundation have come to collect the sofa and television that they're expecting him to donate.
"But then you're a fucking retard, aren't you? You don't have a sense of shame," says Steven, "do you?"
Jake Kilner is extremely unhappy, somewhere in the back of my mind, that his name appears on a list of alleged paedophiles that have been reported to an online vigilante. To Steven, I say nothing.
Penny Clarke hasn't looked over at all so far, but then I'm not surprised, as Steven is right in front of me. Between us, Penny and me. He's putting her off coming and talking to me, he has to be. That's got to be the only reason. Then suddenly I hear a tone. I have an email. My heart almost smashes through my chest when I see it.

Verbal Warning

From: pennyclarke@teleweb.com
Subject: URGENT.

I look over to her and she's looking directly at me! She's actually looking at me. I try to smile but I'm not sure it happens, and Penny doesn't look best pleased with me. I want to tell her I'm sorry for not accepting her friend request. If that's why she's mad with me. Without looking at the email I type up an apology. I tell her that I saw her friend request, I say thank you. I'm sorry I didn't accept it yet I say if that's why she's mad with me. I say I'm going to, when I get on the computer in the canteen. I say if she ever needs to talk she knows where I am. I press send and look at her. Then Steven sees me and follows my eye line to where knows exactly. As soon as their eyes meet, Penny points at him and tells him to check his email. I don't understand. I click on the email she has sent to me and it's by the list of other recipients that I feel faint. all.fu.teleweb.grp@teleweb.com.

Hi all,

I just wanted to set everybody straight on a couple of things about what you've heard from Stevie.

Yes, we slept together. It was quite good. But now I have unwanted guests. It wasn't the other way around. Ladies, please remain well away from Steven Weller, unless you want to take his friends home. I'm sure Zena can back me up.

After Call Work

Regards,

Penny Clarke.

I look at her and she's looking at me, disgust coming over her face. She goes to say something but then Jim is by her desk and she's taken away in the direction of one of the divided-off areas. The Buzz Pods. The whole floor of people is watching. Some laughing. The floor has silence from everybody who isn't on a call. Or laughing. To my left, Steven is bouncing in his chair with laughing. He clicks his fingers or something.
"Oh, fam, that is savage as fuck. I am saving that."
He turns to his computer and starts clicking. He then laughs at me.
"Your bird's going to go viral, mate."

Verbal Warning

Chapter Twelve

Penny

I'm actually shaking with rage. Jim's talking at me. He's asking if I know who I sent it to. I say of course I do. All of the agents. He says no. Not just all the agents. But all the managers, including Zena that I made a serious allegation against, all of the Ops, and the client. He frowns when he says the client, like I'm anywhere near giving a shit. I say but what about Stevie? What about all the shit he's done? Who has he been giving pubic lice to that means he can get away with murder? Jim goes quiet. I know he agrees with me, I can see he doesn't want to be here, but he says Stevie doesn't do anything when everybody's watching. Like the client. I tell him fuck the client. He shakes his head and says he'll let me off with that one, and then he says he'll try to explain it to the bosses. He says I'm floor walking material when I put my mind to it. The patronising bastard. He says to go back and get on the phones. He'll sort it out. I know I'm supposed to thank him here, but it's beyond me today. That prick Stevie has completely ruined my day with this. Seriously. I get up and walk back to my desk, everybody looking at me as I do it. Some girls give me smiles of solidarity which I return gratefully, some of the older ones give me shameful scowls, like I give a shit. Big Barry looks. Oh God. Big Barry. His email. What was that all about? His grovelling apology for not accepting my friend request, like I give anything that even remotely resembles a shit. Honestly, men, even the slightly slow and lonely ones, get over yourselves. It's not always

After Call Work

about you. Obviously, on this occasion, one of your kind is the reason for my rage, but it's not Suicide Clyde over there. In his email he talked about how he's always here if I need him. How tragic must my life be right now that I'm getting pity from Barry. Do you know what I mean? No, but thank you for the very generous offer, Barry. I'll let you know when I hit rock bottom. I can't even look at the guy. I already massively regret friend requesting him. I can't even take it back now in case it tips him over the edge. That email he sent tells me it was a huge thing for him. Basically, unless I want his death on my conscience I'm stuck with him whether I like it or not. I'm going to have to let him in, then phase him out quietly. That's the humane thing to do, surely.

I get back to my desk and unlock my PC. Already there are responses to my email from other people on the floor. Some are messages of support, others are messages with LOL and LMAO etc. Then there are the memes. People using my email profile picture and adding so not funny captions to it. Then there's Barry's.

From: barrybrown@teleweb.com
Subject: Re: URGENT

I am sorry for my last email. You don't have to talk to me ever again. I wanted to tell you that Steven has saved your email. He says you are going to go viral. I can't stop him. He doesn't listen to me. I hate him. I wish he was dead.

Verbal Warning

Yours sincerely.

Barry.

Brilliant. Seriously. This is the last thing I need. I know, I know. I should have thought about this when I sent the email. Yes, I should have, but I didn't. I just needed everybody to know the truth. Now Stevie's planning on showing everybody and their fucking dog my email and taking the piss in all the usual places. He'll paper over the bits where he gave me crabs and will focus on the bit where we slept together. People share this kind of stuff. Then it's all over. For fuck's sake. All this shit for a fuck's sake. I won't bother next time, do you know that? I pause for a brief minute to appreciate my own wit with the bit about for a fuck's sake. I loved it. I amaze myself sometimes. Anyway, seriously, can my life get any worse at the minute? Well. You know now is where something happens to make my life worse than it is at the minute, don't you? It was always going to happen. I get a text. It's from my mum.

We need to talk x.

I ask her if that was meant for me, because I'm not liking the sound of it at all. Whoever that text is for is in for some hell. She replies straight away.

Yea. Come straight home after work x.

I have to ask her what it's about because there's no way I'm going six more hours without going crazy.

After Call Work

Me and you're dad are splitting up. He cheated. X.

And it's as simple as that. I'm up off my seat and people are obviously staring still. I couldn't tell you half of their names. They're just other faces with headsets on. Row on row of people just like me, all with their own personal shit going on. I'm just the latest freak show to pop up. Jim is talking to one of the deputy managers.
"Uh, Jim, can I have a word, please?" I say, chewing on my thumb nail. "In private?"
He tells the DM to watch the floor and takes me to the Buzz Pod.
"Look, Jim, mate. I'm sorry for earlier, seriously. I've got a lot of stuff going on at home and I need to take a half day emergency holiday. It's my mum and dad, there's been something bare weird about the- Look. I can show you the texts if you want?" I'm babbling but I'm only doing him the courtesy of asking for permission before I leave anyway. He knows it and it's up to him whether he wants to be a prick about it. I've already had three absences in the last twelve months. My oldest one drops off record in a week. I hold my phone out to him with the text on.
"You shouldn't be texting on the call floor," he says. I'm actually gutted. I thought he was cooler than that. "I'll say you've had a call," he says with a smile, "get yourself gone."
Oh, Jim. You rascal. I could kiss the old bastard, but elect not to, given my recent track record. I go and tell Amber's concerned face I'm off and that I'll text her later, and then I log out. I avoid eye contact with Stevie

Verbal Warning

and my new, unwanted guardian angel, Barry, as I leave. I feel the burn of eyes all up my back as I do it. Stevie, with his completely fucked up view on life. It's like he's immune to being offended or to the emotional consequences of what he says and does. Barry, through my own conscience and pity for the victim, I've somehow scored myself a new best mate. Amber, my actual best friend. The situation she's set in motion at home through no fault of her own. And the rest of them, watching the fucked up bitch whose life is collapsing all around her walk away. I don't doubt that the rumours have started already. I've been sacked because of the email. The client have overridden Jim's authority and that's me gone. I've walked out through sheer embarrassment at my actions. Believe me, I probably would have, if I didn't need the cash so much. I text my mum to tell her I'm on my way home as I walk over to the car. I hope it's just another blip for them, I really do. I know I'm nineteen and all that, but the thought of them not being together fills me with a dread that actually hurts. I'm back to feeling like I'm six. FML. Seriously, FMFL.

After Call Work

Chapter Thirteen

Barry

I haven't stopped thinking about Penny since she left. I think I caused her to walk out, by telling her what Steven said. Me and my stupid big mouth. But she needed to be told. She needed to know what kind of man he was. So that she could see who she had given her beautiful body to. He's ruining her life like he's ruining mine and I think she is starting to see it now. She's going to miss this meeting that we're queued up to go into, though. It's fine, when I get to the canteen I can log onto Facebook and accept her request and I can tell her everything she's missed. She'll like that, I think. I wish she were here so I could make sure she was okay.

Voices chatter all around me. The people from my team and Jim's team are all bunched around by the door to the conference room. Everybody is talking except me. Steven's stupid commanding voice, begging to be heard over everybody else. Telling the story of how he managed to get Penny into his bed, to Dave with the tattoos. They both laugh and hit their fists together a lot. It's not fair. They shouldn't be talking like that. Not about my friend, not in public, and certainly not in the workplace. Somewhere, in the back of my mind, Jake Kilner is screaming bloody murder at the sky tomorrow morning because he woke up to find that somebody had caught a bus to his village after work and dragged a house key all along the side of his beloved shiny blue car.

Verbal Warning

In the conference room, those who were lucky, pretty, or intimidating enough when the door opened are seated in the twelve chairs around the table. The rest of us are squashed in around the back and sides of the room. At the head of the table is Martin Rose, Patrick's boss. Beside him at one side are Sam and Andy. The client. To the other side are Patrick, and the Senior Learning and Development Coordinator, Lorna. To be honest, out of the five people there, Lorna is the one I like the least. I might not be the brightest bulb in the room, but even I can see she's a nasty piece of work behind the false smile and stylish glasses. I've heard things about her.
"Thank you all for coming today," says Martin. Usually he sounds more Scottish than he does now. "I'm sure you've all been wondering what it's about, just now." There's a murmur of agreement in the room. Martin smiles.
"Of course you have. I would. I'm going to do my best to help you to understand."
Martin stands up from his seat and begins to pace the width of the room. He looks at me. He looks directly at me. My face prickles and must surely be bright red.
"You. What can you tell me about customer centric philosophies?"
I stare at him, wide eyed. I start to speak but he cuts me off.
"Exactly! Nothing! Because it makes no sense! Who could possibly know what having a customer centric philosophy is? How can you be expected to live to it if you don't understand what it means?"
I shrug. His eyes brighten.

After Call Work

"You're on the coal face. The front line. You're the voice of TeleWeb and you're the voice of Sam and Andy, and you're living to philosophies created by outdated and quite frankly pretentious arseholes who liked business speak too much."

There are some laughs when he says a-holes, which he seems to enjoy.

"So that's why, going forward, we're going to be looking for some good people who are capable of blue sky thinking. You are the people giving such great customer service. You should be the ones to tell us how to do it. We need Service Champions. We need people to put themselves on the line to help us to deliver this message. To help us to improve ourselves and our colleagues on a daily basis. Yes?"

Steven has his hand held up, then crosses his arms and leans back in his seat.

"Will there be extra money for doing it?"

A handful of murmurs again. Apparently it was a good question. Ally frowns a little in what looks like disappointment.

"At present, no. This is an opportunity to prove yourself. To make yourself seen. To show that you see the bigger picture. That opportunity is worth more than money and material goods."

Steven tuts loudly and immediately disengages from the situation.

"Can't get pissed on opportunities," he mutters. Some people have a laugh at that. Martin's gaze steels itself as he looks at Steven, whose own eyes scan the room in a show of how rebellious he is. I really really hate him. I'm willing Martin to shout at him, or put him down or do anything to take him down a peg or two.

Verbal Warning

He doesn't. Far from it. He smiles and points at Steven. "It's people like you that we need. Leaders, who aren't afraid to speak out to get everybody over the line. To sell our vision of an army of customer focused, empathetic service soldiers."
Martin waves a hand over all of us and then points to Steven.
"You can all learn a lot from this lad."
Then Martin's face takes a straighter turn.
"That's the good news," he says, "the great news is that these opportunities are available to you in India." Martin then spends ten minutes telling us how they're going to be trialling a team of thirty people working the same pot of customers as us, to support the business in its time of growth. His words, not mine. The Service Champions are to go and assist with sharing our skills and knowledge to build them to our level. That word, opportunities, keeps coming up. It does sound exciting, travelling the world to teach people how to do it, but they wouldn't pick me in a million years. Martin tells us that we should speak with Lorna, as she is the project manager on up skilling our new colleagues in India. That's all the news I need to take my hat out of the ring. Whoever gets the job will be dead in the Ganges with a hundred knives in their back before the first day is done.
"Sorry," says Steven, "but it sounds to me like you're asking for people to go and train our replacements in a cheaper place, for no extra money. Have I got it wrong or is that basically it? Are we looking at unemployment before long?"
Martin shakes his head with a smile.
"No. You'd be training your new colleagues, helping

After Call Work

the business move into new territories."
Martin sits down. A serious look on his face.
"Okay. In the interests of complete transparency. Yes, if the pilot is a success we may look to increase the percentage of FTE in India, but I can guarantee there will be jobs for everybody here. You will all have jobs, so can we please look at the positives? How many people would like the opportunity to join our team in India for three months?"
The arms of half the room go up, including Steven's. Mine stays down. Martin smiles.
"That's why I do this job. To see the passion and ambition of our people. My people. You're all floorwalkers of the future. I guarantee it."

Verbal Warning

Chapter Fourteen

Penny

My mum is on the sofa in her dressing gown when I get home. The television is on but the volume is down. There are crumbs of hard white porcelain or something in the carpet that crunch under my feet. My dad isn't here. My mum's face is red and puffy, which is strange, and upsetting. She never cries. She gets angry and mean and stern and all of that, but she doesn't cry. She looks up at me and her bottom lip goes and her eyes fill up and I can feel myself going too as I scoop down beside her and throw my arms around her. It feels weird. This. Whatever it is. This thing where my mum is the one in need. It doesn't feel right. She cries into my shoulder, her hands digging into me so hard it's uncomfortable. My hand strokes at her blonde hair and I'm not saying anything. I don't know what to say. A tear tickles my face as it pops and drops. What am I supposed to say? It'll be alright? I don't know that though, do I? I'm not going to say something's going to happen when I don't know for sure. I settle for:
"What happened?"
She doesn't say anything for a while, but she tries to calm herself down enough to pull away and look at me. Even when her face is streaming with tears and snot, she's still gorgeous. In comparison, I look like a piglet doing a shit when I cry. She wipes the tears from her eyes, and as she breaks down again she blurts out that my dad cheated on her.
"What? I can't believe that. Who with? How do you

know? What has he said?"
She wails a series of things I can't even begin to decipher from her place on my shoulder. I kiss her head and tell her I'm ringing my dad. If he's actually cheated on her then he's screwed. Once she's got over the shock she'll completely destroy him. I move into the kitchen and my mum's crying fades just enough to be able to hear the ringing tone in my ear.
"Penny," says my dad, monotone and subdued.
"Dad, what the fuck? What have you done? Mum's in bits here."
"Nothing. I've done nothing, Pen. She's got some crackpot idea in her head that I've been shagging around and kicked me out. I'm staying at your nan's until she comes to her bloody senses. Bloody cheating? When does she think I've got time for that, even if I wanted to?"
"Why does she think you've cheated though?"
"She found something."
"What? What has she found?"
"Crabs, in her pyjamas."
My throat tightens. My heart pounds. My fanny itches.
"Crabs, Pen. We haven't had sex in a fortnight. When does she think I've given them to her?"
"TMI, dad. Too much information."
"I think the bitch is turning it back on me because she's the guilty one, because I certainly haven't given her them, so who has?"
Holy fuck. I'm splitting my family up. I'm not. Stevie is. Has. Ladies and gentlemen, we've hit a plot point that sits firmly in my hands. I have a decision to make. I either come clean, and fix this whole mess straight away, or I keep it secret to hide my own shame, at the

Verbal Warning

expense of my parents' marriage. What do you think I do? Of course I do.

"Me," I say, guilt chewing at my stomach like a dog with a half-eaten rubber toy, "it was me that gave them to her."

My dad doesn't say anything for a short time.

"...Pen?"

"I caught them. From a boy at work."

My dad coughs. Then silence.

"...Pen?"

"I've got medicine. I'm dealing with it."

I hear him whimper slightly as he struggles to process the fact that not only has his little girl actually had sex, but she fetched the whole family some souvenirs of the act. How thoughtful.

"Dad, I'm sorry. Come home. I'll clear it up with mum."

I hang up and feel a rush of guilt, and panic hit me. I've given my mum crabs. I don't know how they got from me to her, but they clearly have. She's going to kill me. Ah well, it's just another harsh lesson in what happens if you let Stevie Weller anywhere near you. The bastard is pure poison.

"Mum," I say, sitting down beside her, "I've spoken to dad. He told me what happened."

She wipes away the tears and looks at me. Her face trembling. Her eyes, red raw. I put my hand on her knee.

"He hasn't cheated on you."

"He has. He's got to have. Did he tell you about-"

"The crabs," I interrupt, "yes he's told me about that."

She's watching me hopefully, waiting for the punchline. The evidence that her husband is not a

After Call Work

wanton shagger, prowling the streets looking for sex.
"It's not dad that you've got them from, it's-"
The words stick in my throat. My mum is my hero. She thinks the world of me. I'm her innocent little girl. The illusion is about to be destroyed forever. I'm basically about to tell a five year old that Santa Claus is a mythical creature. Just fucking say it, Penny.
"It was me."
Her head moves back so she can take me in. Her glassy eyes flicker from my face to my hand on her knee, then back again.
"...Pen?"
I sigh. I open my mouth and it just pours out.
"I went home with a boy from work on Thursday. I came home with. With. And he's going round telling everyone it was me that gave them to him but it wasn't so I sent everybody an email and now I'm in trouble at work, and he said he was going to share my email on Facebook so now I'm going to be a laughing stock, and I don't know how you've got them but it wasn't dad. It was me. I'm sorry. Please don't hate me. Please don't split up."
I take a breath. It's out. It's all out. Please make it all better, mummy. Please.
"Oh, Penny," she says, and throws her arms around me. Now it's my turn to sob my eyes out.
"I'm taking medicine," I wail, "I thought I'd got rid of them. I'm sorry."
She puts her hands on my shoulders and pushes me away gently.
"Were you careful?"
"What do-"
"Protection. Did he wear protection?"

Verbal Warning

I nod. She smiles, thankfully.

"Good," she says, "at least that's something."

"I am sorry, mum," I say. She moves tears from my cheeks with her thumbs and kisses my forehead.

"I know, baby girl, but you did a silly thing keeping it all a secret. You caused a lot of trouble. Your dad's not totally blameless, though. If he stopped to appreciate what he had at home instead of checking every other woman and girl out then it wouldn't have been in question. That's not your problem. Who's this boy from work, what's his name?"

So I tell her. I show her pictures of him on Facebook. She agrees that he's good looking, but she says they're the worst kind. She says to aim lower and be treated like a princess. She says not to worry about Stevie Weller. She says she'll take care of it. She kisses me on the forehead and she looks right at me. Her with her beautiful mummy face and me looking like a pig doing a shit. Then she asks if I have any of the crabs medicine left. She says she'll owe me.

After Call Work

Chapter Fifteen

Barry

In the canteen, there are six computers. Of those six, two never work. They're here for us to do personal stuff that we're not allowed to use our work computers for. Usually, I check and engage with the World of Warcraft forums, when I can actually get on the computers. Today, my luck is in. I've got in just ahead of the three o'clock rush, so I've got onto one. I don't bother with the forums today. There's only one destination for Barry, and that's Facebook. I log in to see I have two notifications. One is Penny's wonderful olive branch of the gift of friendship. The other is a private message. I eagerly click at the red dot, hoping to God it's from Penny, to let me know that we're still friends. It's not from Penny. It's from Andrew Benson. Andrew is the tank in my guild. His warrior is called AndGrenade. A tank is basically a character that will make sure the enemy is attacking them and nobody else. A good tank and healer combination can save a dungeon run. Andrew and I are a good tank and healer combination. He's basically my best friend in Azeroth. I choose not to read his message yet, I don't have long on my break so I can't waste time. Instead, I click on Penny's request. Confirm or delete? Confirm or delete? Of course, I don't need to tell you which option I go for. It opens up her profile and I'm straight into her pictures. There are lots of her and her friends in pubs, which isn't really too good. I must have a word with her about her drinking. She's a beautiful person and she could ruin it with that. Already, she's allowed

Verbal Warning

herself to be seduced by him and it can only have been alcohol that was to blame. She's not the kind of person who would do something like that willingly. I move from the drunk pictures. I don't like them. There are other folders that are open to me since I accepted her request. More holiday pictures. I'll look at those at home. I don't want the whole canteen to see her when the people here aren't her friends like I am. I only have six minutes of my break left so I move to send her a message.

Hi Penny,

I hope I didn't offend you today. I didn't mean to if I did. I hope you don't mind me messaging you here, but we are friends now so I'm sure you don't. I wanted to tell you that the meetings today were about India. I mean that they are sending people to India, to help to train people. I know you went home before the meetings but that's what it was about. Steven has volunteered to go so I didn't put your name down. You shouldn't have made sex with him. As your friend I'm sure you don't mind me saying so. If you ever want to go to the park or anything just let me know. I'm always here if you need to talk.

Yours sincerely

Barry

After Call Work

I did put an X but I deleted it. She'll think I'm a blumming creep like Steven. I press send and watch the little tick say she's received it. I wait two more minutes to see if she's seen it yet, but she hasn't, and I have to go back to my desk. The three o'clock rush starts to fill the canteen and people are queuing to get on the computers so I get up from my seat and leave. I hope Penny doesn't take too long to see my message. I try to push my way through the crowds of people that pour into the canteen so that I'm not late back from my break, but there are so many of them. Nobody will let me through. All of them so desperate to get their dinner before everybody else. I say please. I say I'm going to be late. Nobody listens. Somewhere, in the back of my mind, Jake Kilner is frantically calling nine nine nine because somebody set fire to his garden shed. My digital watch tells me I'm already a minute later back than I should be. Then two minutes. I can't afford to lose my job. I can't. Even though I hate it almost as I hate Steven. No. I hate it because I hate Steven. But still. I need to pay my rent. I close my eyes and I push my way through the crowd of people. Bodies move aside and people complain. I meet resistance but I keep going. Then the resistance is gone and I have room to breathe but somebody cries out. I open my eyes and turn to see a girl is on the floor. She has a short skirt on, and I can see her everything as she faces me on the floor. She holds her wrist.
"Watch where you're going, you fat prick," a boy wearing a vest says. It's not a dress down day. I want to say sorry to the girl but I'm late. I turn and I walk away. Behind me the boy wearing a vest says more

Verbal Warning

things. The girl calls me a pervert and tells the boy I looked up her skirt. She says I touched her boobs. She doesn't use the word boobs. The boy calls me a paedophile and follows me. I try to walk faster away from it. My heart beats fast and sweat begins to tickle at the side of my face. I don't turn around but he's there, behind me. He asks me if I get off on feeling seventeen year old girls up. He says I'm a violent sex crime waiting to happen. No, I'm not. Why is it always about sex? What about love? Does nobody believe in love in this place? Penny. I think Penny does. She's lovely. I get to my desk and sit down and I say that I'm sorry I'm late to Darren but he's looking very angrily at me. I feel a push in the back of my shoulder. That word again, paedophile. As I press to put myself into an available state a call comes immediately through. Behind me the angry voice of the boy in the vest asks who my manager is. I don't know if the customer at the other end of the line answers the security questions correctly because I don't listen. Somewhere, in the back of my mind, Jake Kilner is devastated that his dog has been poisoned and will not survive. The boy in the vest takes Darren to one side and angrily points at me. Darren nods and looks to me. In his eyes, I see satisfaction. In my ear the customer asks questions I don't know the answer to. I just say yes. Yes, that's correct. Yes, you can. Yes, that is the balance on your account. Yes. Yes. Steven doesn't have his headset on. He's watching Darren Perry talk to the boy in the vest. He's listening. He turns to me and slides a finger across his throat. He's grinning. My heart bangs and bangs and bangs and bangs and I feel my breath grow lighter and my heart bangs and bangs

After Call Work

some more. In the back of my mind, somewhere, Jake Kilner is attacked by a masked man with a metal pole and left for dead. At the back of my mind, Jake Kilner will talk with a slur for the rest of his life. In my mind, right at the back, somewhere there, Jake Kilner will lose sight in one of his eyes. Darren holds up two hands, palms facing forward, to the boy in the vest. They both nod and the boy in the vest leaves, but not without sneering at me first. Darren comes to my desk and puts my telephone into a state that means I won't take another call when this one is done. He then goes across to speak with Patrick. I am blumming. I really don't like swearing, but I am blumming screwed.

Verbal Warning

Chapter Sixteen

Penny

My mum and dad are locked in the bathroom sharing out the tube of crab killing stuff between them whilst I'm tasked with vacuuming every carpet and fuzzy surface in the house as my first punishment for nearly splitting my parents up. As activities that strengthen a family bond, this must be right up there with appearing on Big Brother, in the embarrassment stakes. My dad couldn't look me in the eye, bless him. He's been in denial about his baby girl's wild ways this whole time, desperate to believe that not a single cock has passed any of the lips on my body. This has just rammed it right home, no pun intended, that I am not quite so innocent as he thought. I've never pretended to be, to be fair to me. I swear in front of both of my parents, and on several occasions I've been drunk enough to pass out at family gatherings. At what point did I give the impression that I would say no to a good shagging? I'm here for a good time, not a long time, so they say. And like my mum said to him when they thought I couldn't hear them, it could have been worse. I could be pregnant, or have bare bad AIDS, or be dead in a ditch. It could have been a hell of a lot worse. Life might be a massive bag of shit right now, but there's always that.

I get a text from Amber when it's time for her to finish work, telling me Barry's been suspended for sexually assaulting a teenager in the canteen. The word on the call floor is that he tried to finger her in a crowd, then

After Call Work

pushed her over when she caught him. They're talking about bringing the police in. That's what the rumours are anyway. The reality will probably be that his arse crack was on show or something. She says she sees that we're mates on Facebook now. She says I should probably look. Oh, for fuck's sake. I forgot to delete my friend request. I forgot about the emails too. How mad was that? He's convinced we're actually friends. I have no idea how I'm going to get out of that without him topping himself. I need to hide it from my timeline before anybody else sees it. My phone's out and Facebook is up. There are fifteen notifications and twenty three messages. It's only now that I realise the scale of what happened today. Not just Barry, but with Stevie and the email I sent too. First, Stevie has tagged me in a photo. You don't have to be Dynamo to know what it is. His photo description simply says I fucked Penny Clarke. She loves a rim job. There are three thousand likes. A thousand comments. Five hundred shares. My email. My fucked up great idea I had to clear my name, come right back to haunt me. Like, seriously, can I get a break here? Can I not just be one of the background characters like Zena who just gives you a basic idea of what a proper cunt Stevie is? Can I please be her? Why am I the poor bitch who gets shit on all of the time? Oh, incidentally, that manager from the client who I shagged that time, he asked if he could shit on me. I said no. Who could possibly be into that kind of thing? This is annoying as fuck. I don't bother to read the comments, it'll be some troll faced keyboard warrior wankers. What's winding me up the most is that my cousins and aunties and all of that lot are friends with me on there. Oh, for fuck's sake. My

Verbal Warning

nannan is my friend on there. I swiftly remove the tag of my name and report the picture, but it's all for nothing really. It's been shared another fifty times since I saw it. I go to the messages and sure enough there are concerned relatives asking me if I've seen it. I go back to the picture he posted. I can't help it. It pisses me off that I'm the one who is coming out of this as the bad one. He's the big fucking stallion superstar, apparently. I won't lie to you, it was good. If he were a footballer and I was a tramp then he'd be getting good reviews on the gossip sites. Four stars. Good with his tongue. Only dropping a star because he gave me fucking crabs. Ohmagod. No, Barry. No no no. You just didn't write that. For everybody to see. Everybody just leave Penny alone, she has a beautiful soul and you are all stupid trolls. I should blumming well kill you all.

Oh my days. We have completely hit absolute, sub-zero rock bottom. What the fuck has he just done to my name?

My mum comes into my bedroom from downstairs. "Your nannan has been on the phone," she says. She sits down beside me. She looks at me, sadness in her eyes.

"I've bare messed up, mum," I say. She puts her arm around me, and hums, like a mm-hmm, as if to say yep, you really have.

"We all make mistakes, Pen," she says as I drop my head onto her shoulder, "I've made my fair share. You should probably not go online for a bit. Let it blow over."

I laugh, bitterly.

"I'm never going on-fucking-line again, ever. This is so

After Call Work

embarrassing. Do you know I accidentally friend requested a lonely bloke from work, and now he thinks we're friends. He's just destroyed everything by being weird in public. I can't go back to work. Not now."

She strokes my hair, and doesn't say much for a short while.

"Be careful around him."

She strokes my hair some more. Stops.

"This boy. Stevie. Where does he live?"

I pull away and look at her, panicked.

"No mum. No. It'll make it a thousand times worse if you go and talk to him. You don't know him. You don't know what he's like."

She smiles, sympathetically.

"I do know what he's like. I've met a thousand like him in my time. I know exactly what kind of boy he is," she says, "and anyway, who said anything about talking?"

I jerk my head back, confused, my eyebrow raised.

"What's that supposed to mean?"

"It means that if he's going to make a fool out of my little girl then he's going to enter a world of pain," she smiles. "Was that too dramatic?"

Verbal Warning

Chapter Seventeen

Barry

Suspended, pending an investigation. That's what they said. It didn't matter that I told them what had actually happened. I was rushing to get back in time from my break, nobody would let me through. I had to push my way through and I must have accidentally bumped into the girl. It was her that had her legs open on the floor. Everybody could see her everything. Not just me. I didn't take photographs. I wouldn't do that. I didn't think she was attractive. Then Darren asked me if I even liked girls at all. He said it was off the record, and Zena didn't write it down. There's no proof that he asked it. Off the record, Darren said that it was probably going to go to disciplinary. He said he didn't fancy my chances. Zena didn't write down that Darren said even if they didn't get me on the sexual assault then I'd had too many chances. I'd been late so many times. I couldn't handle an objection if it was tied down and barely breathing. I couldn't handle an objection if it was dangling from my crotch with two testicles beneath it. He didn't use the word testicles. I was a constant burden. It was all off the record. As he said those things, Jake Kilner was being tortured in his own living room right there at the back of my mind. Jake Kilner and Steven and Darren Perry and the boy in the vest and anybody else that was unkind to me. They were burning and screaming and begging for their lives. It's the only way I can cope with it anymore. They've damaged me. I wished that Penny was there to hear the things he was saying. She is cleverer than I am. She would know what to say and do. Off the record, Darren told me to get help. See a psychiatrist or counsellor or something. He said I had issues. He said he thought that last week, when I tried to, he said he thought it tipped me over the edge. I didn't say that no. No. No. Last week, when I tried to, that WAS me being tipped over the edge by people like him and insults from customers and Steven blumming Weller and people walking around breaking all of the rules and policies and getting away with it but if I get my notebook out once then I am threatened with a disciplinary. The HR department who only seem to exist to help people like Darren get rid of the people he doesn't like, whilst at the same time not in any way helping people to work in a fair and even job. The favouritism. The. The. No. I didn't say any of that. Instead, I sighed, and in the back of my mind, somewhere, and moving slowly to the front, the whole building burned to the ground, taking everybody in it to Hell.

I can't help the tears coming as I sit on the bus home. I wipe them away with the end of my sleeve. A small child three seats away watches me with intrigue. She tells me not to cry. She asks her mummy for a tissue, but the parent ignores her. Up ahead of them, a bald brown man with large headphones moves his shoulders and head to the music he's listening to. The parent has her phone out and is video recording him without his knowledge. He hums whichever tune it is. Even if he caught her doing it I don't know that he'd care. If he did, I don't suppose that he'd do it in the first place. It must be nice to have that as a

Verbal Warning

personality. The ability to not care what anybody else thinks about you. The freedom to act as though you are the only one in a room. Having a knack for hiding from the constant battle in your head between what you'd like to do and what you'd look like to others if you did it. I'm such a loser. Thank God for Penny.

At home I fire up my laptop. It's been five days since I was in Azeroth with my guild. I don't bother to load it up. Instead I go onto Facebook to check my message to Penny. She still hasn't seen it. On my timeline I see that Steven has followed through with his threat to share her email. His vulgar language and vile behaviour sickens me. Then the comments. Oh, no. So many people saying she's a slut. A whore. They say that if she were able to keep her pants on she wouldn't have found herself in this situation. Each comment that says once a dirty slag, always a dirty slag, jabs into my heart and my stomach like a needle. She doesn't deserve this. I write out a comment to them all, and then I delete it. I can't just do that. Steven will hurt me. But Steven doesn't know where I live. He won't see me at work because I have been suspended, pending an investigation. Steven can't get to me here. He won't ever see me again because it's probably going to a disciplinary, and nobody fancies my chances. The comments keep coming, and I can't help reading them. Slutslagbitchwhore. They can't talk about my friend like that. Cuntslagtramp. What gives them the right? Why is Steven the hero in this? He is the one in the wrong. Somewhere, right at the front of my mind, Steven Weller is being kidnapped and held hostage and being starved slowly to death. He is begging me to just let him have a drink of water. A

After Call Work

slice of bread. Right there, in the front of my mind, he is crying and apologising and making false promises to change his ways. I punch out a comment and I press send, and right here and now, I make a silent promise to Penny that Steven Weller will pay for everything he did to her.

Verbal Warning

PART TWO

PENNY

After Call Work

FRIDAY

Verbal Warning

Chapter Eighteen

The doctor looks at me doubtfully. Like the hopeful twinkle in my eye is giving me away. He frowns. Holds the end of his pen towards me. Goes to say something but decides against it.
"Honestly, sometimes I wake up wishing I hadn't," I say, "woken up, I mean," I say, "and sometimes everything suddenly just feels so claustrophobic. I can't breathe and I don't want to feel like that but I do. If I have to go back there now I don't know what I'll do."
He frowns again. I don't tell him it's because I'm hiding from the world of still raw embarrassment of my very public slut-shaming. I don't say it's because my blurred out face and name has been doing the rounds on all of the SOMETHINGBible websites, with the headline of Lad's Response To Email Revenge Is Savage AF. I don't mention that it's because I was trending on Twitter as #rimjobcrabsgirl for several days. I just do a sad smile, a well-practised heavy sigh, and I start to cry. Part of this is genuine. Part of me wants to fall into this old doctor's skinny grandad arms and cry myself dry, but I don't. Instead, I take a tissue and I blow my nose and I smile.
"I just can't go back there, not yet."
He sniffs, and tells me he thinks I should get counselling. He says I've been through a tough time. I should talk to somebody about it, but not the papers. What the fuck?
"Young lady, these things pass. A celebrity will do something stupid and you'll be tomorrow's chip paper

After Call Work

in no time. But I wouldn't be doing my job if I didn't recommend that you sought some help to deal with it."
"What's tomorrow's chip paper?"
"Aside from a great book, it means that they'll wrap your fish supper up today in yesterday's newspapers. They become old news. I don't suppose there's a term for it in the digital age."
I'm a bit weirded out now. My doctor is aware that I love a rim job.
"Can you please just sign me off? The longer the better? Please?"
I've had my five days of self-cert sickness, I need this.
"I will provide you with a medical certificate, I recommend two weeks. But please get help."

The last five days, since you saw me last, have been bare stressful. Facebook took Stevie's picture down after I reported it, but it had been shared and screenshotted that many times that it was impossible to stop. My phone had to stay plugged in to stop from going flat straight away because it was constantly lit up with notifications. Messages from blokes asking me if I wanted to go out, saying they loved rim jobs too (giving and receiving) and from people telling me I was right to do what I did, and from some of Stevie's other girls he'd slept with. And Barry. There's a whole other headache there. It was bare mental.

Verbal Warning

Chapter Nineteen

So on Monday, when I did what I did and then Stevie did what he did, and then Barry did what he did, I got loads of messages from everybody. It did my head in, so I stayed off my phone unless it was people that actually knew me enough to have my number who were texting or phoning me to make sure I was alright. I didn't respond to Snapchat or Instagram or anything, I just watched the fumes of my tank of credibility wisp away out of my life. I couldn't be doing with having to explain myself to people I went to school with who I don't see anymore. People who I went into training with who stayed at work for a week and then left. Barry.

I'd seen that he'd sent me a message after I went home to see my mum, but I didn't read it. I daren't read it because then he'd see that I'd read it and then expect a response. I totally couldn't be arsed engaging with him. You saw his emails and that comment he put on Stevie's original post. There's something actually mentally wrong with him, and already I had feelings of regret about reaching out to him, the same as I had feelings of regret about knocking boots with Stevie. I decided that the best course of action would be to ignore him. If I ever bumped into him in real life I could just say I'd been staying off Facebook until it blew over. I could apologise. But then he started messaging me more. Do you know how you can see the first line of their messages without actually

After Call Work

reading them? Well. Listen to this. Although I never opened them, I screenshotted them to send to Amber.

Monday, eight twenty at night. As your friend I couldn't help.

Monday, eight forty. You don't deserve what.

Monday, nine thirty three. I didn't mean to be so forward.

Monday, ten thirty. I'm sorry if I offended.

Tuesday, eight in the morning. I can't help thinking that you're.

Tuesday, eight thirty. I don't know what to do with.

Tuesday, nine thirty. This song reminds me of you.

Tuesday, ten thirty. I wish you would read my messages.

Tuesday, eleven o'clock. Are you ignoring me? I don't.

Tuesday, dinnertime. I'm going to leave you alone now.

Did he leave me alone? Did he fuck.

Verbal Warning

Tuesday, seven at night. I need to do something about.

Tuesday, nine at night. I'll sort everything out. You'll talk to me.

Then he started liking and commenting on my pictures and statuses. An old status where I first got the job at TeleWeb and was going on about saving up to go travelling. He said he'd love to go travelling with me. A picture of me on holiday on the beach. Big thumbs up to that. The comment just said So Beautiful. The picture of Amber and I at the pub last week. He said he said you didn't need to drink to have a good time. Oh, incidentally:

Wednesday, seven in the morning. Amber is a bad influence.

I just couldn't delete him. I mean, he's obviously tragic as fuck. I just needed a way for him to finally get the message. I didn't mean for it to come out like it did, though. I know, I know. It's just making it worse by stringing him along. I didn't string him along, though. Let's get that clear right now. I didn't do anything. Seriously, I'd only actually spoken to him once at that point. That's not leading anybody on. You can see I let a lot slide, but there became a point where I couldn't do it anymore. It was a whole mess of what the fuck. Stevie, work, the crabs, Barry, and when the fuck would it stop? The FAMbible thing was the tipping point for me. It was just the wrong thing to see at the wrong time. What pissed me off most was that it just glossed over the fact that I was a person, and focused on the fact that I liked a rim job. I could have been anybody. Man or woman. Old or young. They just needed a publicly embarrassing scenario. I gave it to them. Forever more, I am Rim Job Crabs Girl.

So by Wednesday afternoon it started to get to the point where I was getting properly pissed off with Barry's constant messages. Then Amber text me to tell me what was going round. FAMbible. It was there with a couple of lines from my email, a blurred out picture of Stevie, and that headline. At least fifty of my online friends shared it, so it punched me in my face every ten minutes. Winking faces with we all know who this is type comments. Some tagged Stevie, or other friends with comments like this is what I was telling you about. Then Barry messaged me again.

Wednesday, three thirty in the afternoon. He's going to pay for what he's done to you.

So I snapped. I opened up the message. There was no other part of the message. That's all it said. I didn't bother to look at the ones before that. I just tapped out a message at the kitchen table.

Barry, you need to stop messaging me. We're not friends. I requested you to stop you killing yourself, and now you're starting to freak me out. I don't know what I did for you to come on this strong. I'm going to block you, but I want you to get help. You're a broken umbrella away from a killing spree. Take care of yourself Barry.
Verbal Warning

I pressed send after giving it zero thought, but to be honest with you at that point I was donating precisely zero fucks to it either. They could all fuck off. I watched the tick turn to an icon to show it had been read. He started a response. Stopped. Started a response. Stopped. You know where I'm going with this, I presume? After about a minute it all went quiet, so I clicked onto his profile and added him to a block list that now contained about a hundred names, including Stevie. I didn't want anything to do with that shit head, either. I felt bad, though. Then, because do you know what? My life is just that fucked up right now, Barry went and lost his job. Amber said it was for the fingering thing. I don't know if it was before or after I sent him the message, but it probably didn't help his mental state. So if Barry had gone and topped himself now then it was all on me. Whatever I did or didn't do to encourage him, he'd latched onto me and I'd handled it shockingly, like everything else in my life right now.

The next two days calmed the whole thing down without Barry in it. I keep Googling suicides and deaths in our area, fully expecting to hear about him showing up but he hasn't yet. There's still time, it's only been two days. I feel bad saying so, but I wish I'd been mean to him straight away, instead of letting his weird little thing that he has with me grow into apparently quite a weird big thing. It's been a weight off my mind. It has taken the edge off of the whole thing. Despite what I tell my doctor, I do feel a little better. It's going to be a while before I'm ready to go

After Call Work

back to work, though. Especially with Stevie, and Rim Job Crabs Girl hanging over me. Aside from that one message to Barry a couple of days ago, I'm still not responding to anything. I just sit and sigh and watch a thousand people I'll never know chatting shit about me, and I force myself not to bite back.

Verbal Warning

Chapter Twenty

Amber shows up at mine some time after eight with a bottle of vodka and her iPod. We're not going out, fuck that. I'm not ready for that. Not yet. If you put alcohol in me and set me loose on a world that's bare taking the piss out of me somebody is going to get banged, and I can't be held responsible for it. So Amber's come round here to fill me in on the outside world and its dirty laundry. I haven't seen her since Monday, and I'm buzzing when I see her gorgeous face. We go straight up to my room; it's still pretty tender downstairs. No. Not that downstairs, the lotion fixed that. I mean my mum and dad. They had a massive talk and went for a bit of a date night last night, and as far as I know they're sleeping in the same bed but there's still a very slightly edgy vibe around them. They don't need the sexy cat goddess that is my best friend sitting like a stunning elephant in the room. No. You know I'm not trying to say Amber's fat. There's more meat on a butcher's pencil, as my dad says.
"You'll be happy to hear that Stevie didn't come to work today," says Amber as she flicks away at her iPod, she frowns, "I put a playlist together, but I've lost it."
"Good," I say, "the Stevie thing, not your playlist. I hope he's dead."
She laughs morbidly.
"Barry probably killed him after they sacked him."
I laugh in mock horror.
"Ohmagod. You could be right. He's probably made Stevie pay for what he did to me."

After Call Work

We laugh, but it did cross my mind as soon as she said it. It's highly unlikely though. Stevie would eat Barry up and spit him out. The truth of it is Stevie no doubt got hammered last night and woke up in somebody's bed, leaving them nothing but pubic lice and a sore fanny as reminders of his time between their legs. He no doubt couldn't be arsed with going home and getting ready for work so he text Darren to tell him he wouldn't be in today. That, is what will have actually happened. Eventually Amber finds her playlist and the first tune on is Rihanna. She finds a volume she's happy with and sets her iPod down. I don't mind her taste in music, to be honest. She likes the crowd pleasing tunes, modern ones we all know and can have a dance to. I get my taste in music from my dad, so I'm more into the old Motown type stuff. Don't get me wrong, there are some bangers in the charts now, but I'll always have a weakness for Motown. Sunday afternoon play of my dad's vinyl record of the Supremes? I love it.
"The doctor signed you off then?" Amber asks as she dumps herself in my big bean bag within touching distance of the iPod. She loves controlling the music at any social gathering where there's chance to control the music. It makes her happy, so why not?
"Yeah, two weeks. I might be ready to come out from my cocoon by then."
"Look, mate. You're the queen of that place. How much shit do you think you're going to get? You think Brenda with the limp is going to give a fuck about it? The quicker you come back the better. I've been bored without you."

Verbal Warning

I give her an affectionate smile. Grateful that she still cares. That's what a good friend does to you. Melts the shit away, if only for a few seconds.

We chat all night, talking mostly about work and the people there. She tells me that Brenda with the limp has got in trouble for telling the client that TeleWeb are a shit employer. She didn't say shit though. She did the thing that Brenda does where she'll make sly digs that aren't that sly. I'm surprised they let the client listen in to her, to be honest. She's always been the same. Any time there's a meeting with management she'll always bring it round to the state of the toilets or how there's no hand sanitiser when you want it. Honestly, we once had a man come in from a company that teaches you about the products we're supposed to be promoting. Brenda spent a full hour bitching about the quality of the toilet paper we're given. I don't mind her. Sometimes she provides welcome diversions. Amber tells me that Tony has been picked to go to India to train them to do our jobs. She says they're still accepting applications if I fancy it. It does sound appealing, even just as a taster of the wider world, but there's no chance that they'd pick me. I'm trouble in tight clothes. She asks if I want her to put my name forward to Lorna.
"Lorna's in charge?" I say. "She hates me since I shagged Gareth that she was into. No chance of me getting it then."
This is true. Lorna is a wannabe corporate bitch with an unhealthy relationship with cocaine. She's all suits and PowerPoint presentations at work but she's an animal when she's out and on the coke. I know for a

fact she's shagged Darren Perry and Patrick. There's nothing wrong with that, but the cynic in me says she did it for professional gain rather than for the carnal pleasure. It's worked out for her so far, but there's got to be only so far you can get on joyless shagging without actually being any good at your job. Gareth was a head of department last year. Lorna had got her eyes on him, but he'd got his eyes on me, so what could I do about that? Anyway, she's hated me ever since. Haters gonna hate, so they say. No. You could put me on Bondi Beach with my tits out and a Pina Colada in my hand, I'd love it. Slide Brown Nose Tony and Lorna into this picture and you've ruined my holiday. I'm not going to be applying for a trip to India. Tony will love it though. He was a boring wanker before, I bet he's insufferable at work now. Off to teach a bunch of people to do his job, without realising that as soon as they can do his job, he won't have a job. No matter what bullshit stories they spin about us always having jobs. Did you notice how it's not that we'll have our jobs? We'll just have jobs. Non-specific. We're not as stupid as they think we are. Most of us, anyway. I know, I know. I was stupid enough to accidentally inherit lice, a stalker and a catchy nickname, who the fuck am I to judge the intelligence of others? It's a different kind of intelligence that I'm talking about, though. Ironically, I'm not sure which kind exactly that I'm talking about. I'm blaming the vodka.

The rest of the night, we spend laughing and dreaming up stupid ways to get back at Stevie. We have our phones out, then it kind of becomes a blur. My dad

Verbal Warning

comes in. Amber says hi in a filthy way because I told her about him checking her out last week. He just looks at the floor and says it's getting late and to keep it down. She giggles and says sorry. He leaves. I have my phone out some more and then I wake up. It's half past two, and I'm in my pyjamas on the bed. On top of the sheets. Amber is in my bed, sleeping. I shuffle my bum around until I'm under the sheets with her, and I reach across and feel for my friend's hand. She doesn't stir, and is completely unaware of how much she means to me right now. I close my eyes and I sleep.

After Call Work

SATURDAY

Verbal Warning

Chapter Twenty One

The dying animal screech of my phone hitting low battery levels rips me awake some time around still-dark o'clock. Amber stirs beside me but continues to snore lightly. My mouth is dry and claggy. I take my phone to the toilet with me. Without turning in the light I lean over the bathroom sink and slurp eagerly at the cold water tap, quietly gargling it to breathe life into my dying, furry tongue. Placing my backside onto the cool toilet seat I let my bladder pour piss loudly into the water beneath me. I unlock my phone, but I'm far too tired for my brain to choose an app to open. It's just that I've got so used to sitting here with it entertaining me during toilet times that it's grown to be a comfort thing. I guess. I don't know. I scrunch up some toilet paper and I wipe. Some wee goes on my thumb but it's okay. I step back to my bedroom and slide in beside Amber. My phone wails at me again. Begs me to pump it full of sweet electricity. My hand reaches to the side of the bed, blindly searching for the wire. As I plug it in I see more notifications. All of the usual places. I need to sleep, but I need to see. My thumb opens Facebook. Fifteen notifications. My thumb opens them. The top one says that some people I don't know like my post on the Call Centre Problems page. The second one says some people I don't know commented on my post on the FAMbible page. The third one says Amber likes my status. I don't remember writing anything. They must be old. I sleep again.

After Call Work

Oh. Fuck. I wake with a start when it's now-light o'clock. What did I do? Flashes of Amber and I giggling. Both of us taking turns to hold my phone and write something. Snapchat. Instagram. Twitter. We were everywhere. Stevie's Instagram. What did we do on there?

"Morning," says Amber's squeaky, just awake voice. I turn to see her smiling a naughty smile at me, her phone unlocked in her hand. "We've been bad."

I knew it. My hand rubs at my left eye, like it always does when I get one of those awful uncomfortable feelings of shame at my drunken actions. My hand moves across to rub my right eye as the sense of shame grows.

"Oh my days. How bad?"

She holds her phone up. On the screen, I'm there in all my glory. Fully clothed but holding my vibrator between my legs. The caption says *Stevie Weller can suck my fuckin dick*. The picture is on Instagram, and he's been tagged in it. I have to stifle an unexpected giggle, because I remember doing it now. Amber and I were joking about paying somebody to kidnap and bum Stevie to death. We were doing silly gangster voices saying we were going to murderbum him. *Stevie Weller, I'm here ta moydabahm yah*. It was probably funnier at the time.

"Has he commented?" I ask, my gut churning in anticipation of what other crap I've put out online. Amber shakes her head, no.

"What did we put on Facebook?" I ask. I know something is there but daren't look at it. She grins a wicked grin.

"Don't you remember any of it?"

Verbal Warning

"No, I remember my dad coming in and asking us to be quiet. After that it's a bit of a blur."

She spins her phone around. The same picture and caption. It's on FAMbible, the Call Centre page, VIRALbible, yada yada. We posted it everywhere. Then Amber went round tagging him in it. There are a few dozen likes on each of them. Some comments, but weirdly there's nothing from Stevie. He's usually the kind of wanker that likes to get the last word in, and our daft games are hardly enough to send him burrowing underground like the worm he is. It is only early, though. He'll surface soon, I'm sure of it. There's another doubt that's scratching at my brain, though. On top of this uneasy notion that Barry has done something stupid in my name, there's something my mum said. She said she'd sort it out. She said she'd sort him out. Oh gosh, what if she's killed him? Where Barry would get chewed up and spat out by Stevie, my mum would completely annihilate Mr Weller without missing a single heartbeat. She's very protective of me, and so is my dad. I'm their only baby. There are a few reasons, or motives, as they say. They got crabs from me and I got them from Stevie. The Facebook stuff. His behaviour in general towards me since we shagged. The fact that my Auntie Melanie asks how I am by referring to me as Rim Job Crabs Girl. My Auntie Melanie is only three years older than me, and she is a stone cold slut. I'm not judging, I love a dick as much as the next girl. And rim jobs, of course. Anyway, she's my dad's sister. I might have once shagged one of my potential uncles when she was zoning in on him at a club in the city, so she's not my biggest fan. All of these factors point to the possibility of my parents being

After Call Work

murderers. Again, in my name. I could really do without this. If Stevie is dead because of me I will do my nut.

"What's up, babes?" Amber asks. I've been quiet for a while. I watch her big sexy cat eyes peer down on with concern. The morning sun illuminates the emerald green in them and it strikes me just how naturally gorgeous she is. She's so lucky. If she weren't my best friend I would definitely be tempted to dabble in the dark art of lady love with this girl. I'm sorry. Delay tactics.

"What if something's happened to Stevie? Something doesn't feel right. He would have definitely responded by now." I say. She smirks.

"So what if it has? He deserves it. He's a prick."

"I mean it, Am. What if he's dead because of me?"

"Death by Barry as a crime of passion? I doubt it. The only thing that's died is Stevie's phone. He'll be back, being a wanker before you know it," she says, "and anyway, even if Barry did do something, it's not your fault. He's a fucking nutter. You're lucky he hasn't decided to kill you instead. If he can't have you then nobody can, you know?"

I feel sick through a combination of emotions and last night's vodka. I don't tell her my fear that my parents may be murderers. I can't.

Verbal Warning

Chapter Twenty Two

Amber leaves an hour later, giving me a hug and a kiss and telling me not to worry. She'll text me if she hears anything and she'll let me know when Stevie shows up to work on Monday. I can't wait until Monday.

I sit at the kitchen table. My phone has an unsent text on the screen, the flicker of the cursor awaiting further instructions taps at the corner of my eye. The text says *Are you alive dickhead?* and the number it will go to if and when I send it, belongs to Stevie. I probably won't. What if he's dead? What if the police see it and then think I sent it to cover my arse? Ask a dead guy if he's alive, the perfect ruse. I've considered withholding my number and just phoning him and hanging up, but can they trace it? Oh God. The pictures. The Internet is full of me waving a dildo around saying a very possibly dead boy can suck my dick. If he's dead then. I don't know. He gets one last kick into my teeth by being the poor murdered innocent, taunted by a spurned lover (me) who definitely killed him in a crime of passion. I grab my phone and delete this message as my mum comes into the kitchen.
"Morning," she says, "has Amber gone?"
"Mm-hmm."
"How are you feeling? Tender?"
Oh, mummy, tender is just the start. Tender is a dizzy head and an unease in my belly. Tender is the dream I dream of. How I'm feeling is confused, nauseous, scared and not just a little pissed off that in one way

After Call Work

or another somebody I know has murdered somebody else I know in my honour. Probably.
"Mm-hmm," I say. I look at my phone's wallpaper. A selfie of me at the zoo in front of a giraffe with its head bobbing down a bit. I bare love giraffes.
Mum doesn't say much, just goes turns the cold tap on and fills a bottle with some juice. She's dressed for running. She loves exercising. I don't know how she can be bothered, but it's working for her all over. She's bare toned, my mum.
"I'll see you in a bit," she says as she passes and kisses me on the top of my head. I don't know if the kiss somehow felt more suspicious than usual. Firmer. Like secrets. I know, I know. I'm being mental, but what the fuck? How can she just go off for a run when she might have killed Stevie? Because she didn't, I know. I get it. I'm being paranoid. She didn't kill him and neither did my dad. He's not dead. She's just warned him off me at most. That's what it will be. He didn't go to work because he's got a black eye or something off my dad. Or more likely, my mum. The reason he hasn't responded is because he's on a warning. That sounds and feels a lot better. That sounds and feels like relief. But what about Barry? What has he done? For fuck's sake. I let out a sigh, and pick up my phone. I simply text to Stevie, *we need to talk.*

I leave my phone in my bedroom and take a shower. I don't look at it whilst I dry and straighten my hair. I don't touch it whilst I put on my make-up. I ignore it whilst I get dressed. I refuse to. Because I won't be ruled by that prick. When Stevie responds, I'm just

Verbal Warning

going to tell him I got the wrong person, and then I'll tell him to fuck off. I'll tell him to delete my number.

An hour later and I'm in the car on my way to Stevie's house. He hasn't responded.

Ten minutes later I'm outside the shit hole that he lives in. It's basically a squat. His housemate Luke sleeps on an airbed on top of a mattress on the floor. The downstairs of the house is all stains and beer cans. Cocaine dust on the coffee table between playing cards and poker chips. Stevie's bedroom is slightly nicer. It's a large attic room with a low leather bed. He's obviously got a red lamp, because he's a clichéd prick. His bedroom wall is graffitied in that way that says he thinks it makes him look cool. He got his mate in to do it in exchange for some M-Cat. It does look cool, in a derelict house heroin den kind of way. The same mate probably does the same thing on the walls of local community centres for a few hundred pounds of council money. His room smelled. It smelled of damp clothes and vinegar sweat. And sex, a few hours later. How long ago it feels by now.

I stride up to the door and I knock. Hard. The street is fairly quiet, with only a middle aged guy strolling back to wherever with a newspaper under his arm and a bottle of milk in his hand. He sucks on one of those electric cigarettes and blows an unnecessarily dense cloud out as he passes and smiles at me.
"Morning," he says cheerfully. I don't get any sleazy vibes from him so I mumble a response and give him a weak smile. I knock again. Behind the glass, there's

After Call Work

movement. My heart dances a tango inside my chest as my fears of a dead wanker edge closer to obliteration. Be him. Please, be him. The door opens. What stands there is not an arrogant prick with an obscene lack of empathy for anybody. What stands there is a small weaselly boy with a ragged beard and a beanie hat. Beneath his face is a thin body, covered in tattoos and clothed in a flannel shirt and baggy boxer shorts. His equally thin dick sneaks a look at me through the loose hole in the front of them. He catches me looking at it and smiles.
"Sometimes, it's hard to contain such a monster."
He takes a pull on a roll up cigarette and smiles again.
"I assume you're Luke," I say, shifting my eyes from his pecker to his face. He nods and puts the cigarette to his lips before pointing it at me, his teeth showing through his happy grin.
"I know who you are," he says. "You love a rim job."
Of course he knows who I am. I don't doubt that Stevie has told everybody whose path he crosses all about his part in my humiliation. I cross my arms.
"Where is he? Is he in?"
Luke shakes his head.
"No, he hasn't been home since Thursday," he says, but it sounds like lies. I huff a massive sigh and if you thought I wouldn't push my way past him into the den of filth to see for myself then you obviously haven't seen or read enough woman-on-a-doorway scenes in your lifetime. I'm hardly going to turn and take his word for it, am I?
"He's not in, I told you," moans Luke behind me.
I move quickly into the living room. The light of day shows just exactly how grim it is. The carpet is a shiny

Verbal Warning

and pushed-down layer of scum, where drinks have been spilled and stepped in and dried on top of drinks that have been spilled and stepped in and dried. The sofa has a hundred circles of spilled fluid stains. There's an ashtray that has nothing but dismantled cigarettes and butts. Beside that a plastic video case has a ball of weed waiting to be smoked. Luke steps into the room behind me, and closes the door.
"I told you he wasn't here," he says, "but you're welcome to stay."
I feel his presence edge closer to me than would ever be considered appropriate. Then it happens. At first I thought it was a finger poking at my arse cheek, but as I turn and move away from him I see his thin dick standing to attention. He leers at me.
"What the fuck are you doing?" I say. I try to look him in the eye, but he makes his dick bounce up and down without touching it. Danny from work calls it doing a dick dance. His grin spreads, the roll up cigarette between his teeth. I can see why he and Stevie get on.
"Seriously, put it away or you're going to lose it."

I leave the house having checked each of the scummy, and more upsettingly, empty rooms. Luke was still on the floor trying to coax his testicles from somewhere in his lungs when I left. Seriously though, what is it with men and boys? You get a woman on her own, and what? It's open season on her vagina? Fuck off, would you? If and when I want it, I'll be very clear about that. Until then, the only place you're shagging me is in your head.

After Call Work

Chapter Twenty Three

I can't go home. Not yet. So I drive. The radio plays chart stuff that fades into nothing and every short haired man on the street becomes Stevie, so I slow down and then it isn't Stevie. Then beeps. Cars, honking their horns at me to get a move on. The first five or six times I raise my hand to apologise. Beyond that, they get a middle finger. Fuck them. I've had enough shit on my plate this last week to feed every fucking fly on the planet. Somebody honking their horn is nothing to me, or anybody else. Don't they know they're honking at the famous Rim Job Crabs Girl?

I scan through my hands free phone book on the digital display on the dashboard. I find his number and I dial. The inside of my car is filled with the monotonous and repetitive sound of me outbound calling. It hits the answer machine and I hang up and hit redial. The act becomes a second nature broken record before long. I barely acknowledge the road before me and move only forward until there is nowhere else to go but left or right, and then I go forward until there is nowhere else to go but left or right. Repeat to fade. Stevie obviously has no intention of picking up the phone. Either through choice or lack thereof. But I have no intention of letting him get away with doing this to me. He isn't dead and he will pick up. Eventually. I hope.

Verbal Warning

Before long I'm at a dead end. The leisure centre with the ice rink that we used to come to when I was at school. Friday night disco night, it was called. Beneath the brrrrrrr brrrrrrr of me calling Stevie I look at the kids and their parents pouring into the leisure centre. All bags and towels for going swimming and not a care in the world on their Saturday afternoon. Brrrrrrr brrrrrrr. Oh, to be ten again. I know, I know. You're nineteen, Penny. Get a fucking grip. You wouldn't know hardship if it grabbed both of your nipples and twisted them bare savage. Brrrrrrr brrrrrrr. Well I'm going to beg to differ, here. When you've gone slut shame viral, then you can make a call on how hard I've had it. No pun intended. Brrrrrrr brrrrrrr. When the whole country is laughing at you and not with you. Brrrrrrr- The person you are calling cannot take your call at the moment. When the one person who caused all of it is the only one who can make everything alright, just by not being dead, it's a shit state of affairs. To re-record your message, just press hash at any time. Fucking hell. What I wouldn't do for a hash key on my life in this last week. Some way of re-recording the whole lot of it. There isn't though, is there? You just have to make your mistakes and live with them. I guess it's up to you how you learn from them. If, you learn from them. Brrrrrrr brrrrrrr. Brrrrrrr brrrrrrr. Brrrrrrr brrrrrrr. Beep. Beep. Beeeeeeeeeeeep.

I smash the steering wheel hard and scream louder and louder and louder. Some kids getting off a bus nearby look at me and laugh. Brrrrrrr brrrrrrr. The person you a calling cannot take your call at the

After Call Work

moment. Where the fuck are you, Stevie? I feel my body begin to tremble, from my fingers wrapped loosely around the wheel, up my arms and into my shoulders. It reaches my bottom lip and then the tears start. I almost wish Stevie were dead, just so that I'd know what the hell had happened to him. I can't stand the not knowing. The mystery. I cry myself stupid, here in the car park of the fucking leisure centre. My phone rings. My mum. I don't answer for a while as I try to compose myself, sniffing away the snot that's bubbling away in my nose. I press to answer.
"Hi mum," I say to the air around me in the car. She doesn't say much. She doesn't say anything. Not for a few seconds anyway.
"Pen? Are you okay? Are you crying? Why are you crying?"
Her worried voice booms from every speaker in the car, panic at my current state of mind. An elderly couple walk past and give me a disapproving look for no reason whatsoever. The old man continues to look back at me. I wind my window down.
"Why don't you take a fucking picture? It'll last longer," I call out to him in a rage. He turns away.
"Who? Pen what's happening?" The voice of my mum asks from every speaker in the car.
I shake my head as if she's here with me and I say nothing. Nobody. I ask what she wants. I don't mean it to come out like I do but it just spills out of my mouth that way and I instantly feel bad. I apologise. I say yes, I have been crying but I'm okay. Life's just getting me down.
"You need to come home, love," she says, "the police have been round looking for you," she says, "they need

to ask you some questions. They mentioned that boy, Steven."

My world, once again, comes crashing down around me. They found a body. They've seen the pictures of me saying he can suck my dick and they've put all sorts of twos together,

"I didn't kill him," I blurt out, "I thought you did."

Silence.

"You said you were going to sort him out and then he's disappeared and I thought you killed him."

Silence.

"Mum, did you kill Steven?"

Silence. And then.

"No, Penny, I did not kill him. The police wanted to ask you questions about an assault on his housemate. Penny, you need to come home right now."

Silence.

"Penny? I said come home. Now!"

Silence.

"Where are you? I'm coming to get you."

My mum's voice, from every speaker in the car, tells my dad to get his trousers on. Her voice asks me again where I am. I tell her quietly. She says to stay here and hangs up. I turn off the engine and I get out of the car. I lock it. I walk away from it, toward the leisure centre. I don't go in, I just stand at the window that looks down over the ice rink where I used to spend my Friday nights with Sophie and Frankie from school, eagerly gliding over the ice, looking for equally eager boys to get off with. I remember I once snogged six lads in the same night. Added them all on Facebook and watched with glee as they each liked everything I posted, all under some impression that they were my only

After Call Work

conquest of the night. Over time they faded away, replaced by others who came along. Then snogging turned to shagging, and shagging turned to this. God, I fucking hate adulthood. A young girl holds hands with a boy as they slowly edge around the big ice rink. He's unsteady on his feet but she keeps him securely upright, and every now and then they stop to cuddle. He nudges himself to the edge and she glides around, turning to skate backwards, but she never takes her eyes from him. He looks so happy just to watch her. Proud that she's got these skills and even prouder that she's his girlfriend. They make me sick.

God. There's something bare wrong with me.

Verbal Warning

Chapter Twenty Four

The wall of the police station waiting room is a collage of telephone numbers to report things to. Anonymously, of course. Violence; domestic, sexual, drunken, fatal, yada yada. Drugs; smack, crack, weed, speed, yada yada. Theft; property, money, yada yada. Missing persons; loved ones. Stevie.

Beside me my mum's sitting, her hand grips tight to my hand on her knee. My dad took my car home and is no doubt back in his pants in front of Soccer Saturday with a betting slip in front of him. He'll have his phone on loud, though. Just in case.
In the car over here my mum kept on at me. Why did I think she killed Stevie? Why did I think Stevie was dead? I didn't say much. Just stared out of the window and watched the town move by. She kept asking and asking these questions but I was too far gone into my mental cave to provide any logical answer to any of them. I didn't even care about this shitty allegation that the bearded weasel Luke has made about me assaulting him. I still don't. It's bullshit. I'm sure they can find DNA from the tip of his rancid penis on the cheek of my arse.

Obviously this means my mum's probably out of the frame for Stevie's murder. You can't fake the kind of horrified look she gave me when I asked her in person about her involvement, and now I'm putting Barry right back into the frame. I don't know where Barry

After Call Work

lives, thankfully. If I did I'd be. Ohmagod. I *do* know where Barry lives. Not off the top of my head but he told me, in the first email he sent to me. When he was saying sorry for not accepting my friend request. When he told me I could go round and talk to him any time.

"I need to go to work," I say, my right knee suddenly bouncing away. I pull my hand out from under my mum's and stand up. "I need to check my emails." My mum stands up too, a worried look on her probably not a murderer face. She's about to say something but then a voice calls out my name. We both turn to see a youngish blonde woman smiling at me. She can't be more than a few years older than me. She's petite and pretty. Here, with what can only be described as a proper job. I don't even mean compared to my piece of shit, stress for pennies station in life. You've got to have some steel in you to be a policewoman. I try to smile back but can't. I want to leave now. I need to see my emails. I need to see Barry. He's my only chance at knowing that Stevie isn't dead because of me. I can't leave. I'm ushered through the door and down some corridors and into an interview room.

"Thanks for coming in," she says as we all sit down. Me and my mum on one side of the table, her on the other. She doesn't put any tapes in the player and she doesn't say the date or anything. She just has a notebook in front of her. "I'm PC Jen Hoyland, and I'm sure your mum has told you why we needed to speak with you."

"That sleaze bag says I assaulted him," I say, "did he tell you he got his dick out at me?"

Verbal Warning

PC Jen Hoyland frowns at me. Whether it's because this is news to her or because I said dick, she doesn't say.

"I went round to talk to Stevie Weller. He wasn't there and Luke closed the door on me and poked me in the arse with the end of his skinny dick, so I kicked his balls. There's not much more I can say than that."

"Steven Weller. This is the boy who," she says, looks at some notes, looks at me, looks at the notes, looks at me again, recognition in her eyes that threatens to derail her until now professional behaviour.

"I'm Rim Job Crabs Girl," I say without humour, letting her off the hook, "and yes. He is the boy who."

"I'm sorry," she says, a sympathetic edge to her voice, she sounds genuine, "for what happened to you."

"Me too."

She clears her throat. Our moment of tenderness a thing of the past.

"So why did you go to see Mr Weller?"

Here. Right here at this point. This is where I'd like to be able to tell you that I told this police officer all about how I think Stevie's dead. This is where I could get somebody else to do all the work and the worrying. Only, I didn't. I just looked at my mum and then at PC Jen Hoyland and I said I wanted to talk to him. He'd not been answering my texts or calls and I wanted to scream at him. I wanted to hit him and tell him how he'd ruined my life. At this point, PC Jen Hoyland's eyebrows go up, and she looks at the notes again.

"So, you're saying that you went to his address in an aggressive mood, only, you didn't find Steven, so you assaulted his housemate instead?"

After Call Work

"No. I went to argue with Stevie, and his housemate was assaulted because he thought that forcing his erect dick into my personal space was an effective seduction technique. Don't twist what I'm saying, please."
"Do you think your recent very public activity and admissions may have given Luke Harris the impression that you might respond to such behaviour?"
And there it is. I deserved to be sexually assaulted without defending myself because I enjoyed sex with the wrong person. I look at this police officer before me as disgust takes me over.
"I'd like to go now," I say to my mum.
"But we haven't-"
"Yes. Yes we have," my mum says as I stand up and walk to the door. "You should be ashamed of yourself."
They carry on talking, my mum with her raised voice and the police officer with her trying to stay calm but I don't hear words, and then I don't hear anything else except me crying.

Verbal Warning

Chapter Twenty Five

My rapid descent from grace continues, and I can't find the emergency stop button. There is no brake. There isn't even a tree branch anywhere to force into the front spokes of my freewheeling trip to the lower levels of rock bottom. Just when I think life can't take anything else from me it pulls away another dusty sheet, swings its arm and launches another few shreds of my dignity into the abyss. You could be forgiven for thinking I'd shagged that bitch Karma's husband in her bed and sent her a video of it on WhatsApp.

I'm not being arrested or anything yet, but I'm told not to take any holidays, in case the police need to speak with me again. They need to speak with Luke again, about the dick prodding thing.

My mum won't take me to work from the police station without a full explanation as to why, and it's going to be too late to drive there myself by the time we get home, so I slump in my seat in the car and chew at the skin around my thumb nail, watching my own slanted reflection in the passenger side window.
"I'm worried about you, Pen," my mum says.
"So am I," I reply.
I really am worried about me. I'm worried that this is my life now. My present and my future tainted by my past. I've sunk so very low that there are nothing but solid and smooth walls around me and no matter how much I strain my eyes above me there is no light.
"I don't think you're dealing with this very well. I wish

After Call Work

you'd talk to me about it. I might be able to help."
But you're a part of the problem, my wonderful
mummy. Saying that you'd deal with Stevie, right
before he disappeared. If you hadn't, then it would
only be Barry and I could have told you everything
and we could have sorted it out. I pull out my phone
and push the blue square with the white F. I find my
blocked list and I find Barry and I unblock him. I find
Stevie and I unblock him too. Stevie's last post was
Thursday. I'm getting bare pussy tonight fam. Nothing
since then. Barry's last post was Thursday, too. A
picture of a cat with a dead mouse hanging from its
mouth. The caption says Take Control. I gasp in pain
as I chew too deeply into the skin around my thumb.
Fuck this. I tap out a message to Barry, ignoring the
hundreds that he's sent to me. Ignoring the one I sent
to him. I simply write I know what you've done. Send.
The circle turns to a tick. The tick turns to Barry's
cartoon wizard profile picture. Then the bouncing
circles. He's responding. What have I done? I write it. I
write what he's done. You've murdered him. Circle,
tick, profile picture. No reply. I give it a minute of no
response and I tap out another message. You killed
him didn't you? Circle, tick, profile picture. Bouncing
circles. A response. It wasn't me. My heart stops. It
wasn't me. It wasn't you, Barry, but you know who it
was? Is that it? It wasn't me. That's not something you
would say if you didn't know. Is it? No. You'd say what
the fuck are you on about? Who have I killed? Get your
facts a hundred percent straight before you go
throwing accusations like that around. You don't say it
wasn't me. You're not Shaggy.

Verbal Warning

When we get home, my mum calls after me that we need to talk as I go up the stairs two at a time to my bedroom. I pull out my laptop. I could get into a lot of trouble for what I'm going to do. I signed a policy, amongst about fifty other policies, to say I wouldn't access my work emails from anywhere but work. I remember rolling my eyes and making a comment about why would I ever want to access them at home? They sacked a girl a few months ago for it. She was a floorwalker who kept telling everyone she was a deputy team leader. She even had business cards made up. Anyway, she kept accessing her emails from home on her days off in case there was something that she'd missed out on. Eventually they clocked it and she clocked out permanently. Right now, I don't give anything like a fuck about whether I get sacked or not. I haven't been there for a week, I could quite easily forget I work there at all. I sign in to my account and scan the hundreds of irrelevant messages. Stuff about India, some messages from Tony, all of them with URGENT before the actual subject. URGENT - Floor Standards. URGENT - Employee Engagement Survey. URGENT - Matthew's Leaving Collection. Blah blah fucking blah, Tony. You're so fucking *boring*. His tediousness gets me down. How can somebody get through life being so irritatingly dull? Barry's email is about eight pages in, and it sits right next to the mistake of a message I sent to everybody. I know that one word for word. I pull his email up.

From: barrybrown@teleweb.com
Subject: I'm sorry

After Call Work

Dear Penny,

I'm sorry if I made you mad by not accepting your friend request on Facebook this weekend. Thank you for the gift of your friendship. It means the world to me. I've been really busy with dungeons and I lost track of time. I'm sure you know how it is. I promise I will accept it later when I can get on a computer in the canteen. If you ever need to talk to anybody then you know where I am. My address is flat six, 28 Furnivall Street, if you would ever like to come and play MMORPG's with me. You would make a beautiful Night Elf. I'm sorry again for ignoring you accidentally. I would never do it on a purpose.

Yours sincerely,

Barry.

What the hell is he talking about? Dungeons? Elves? What's with the yours sincerely all the time? He's a straight up, grade A fruitcake. I don't have time to ponder it too much, because I have somewhere to be. I'm finding out once and for all what he's done. He can tell me himself and I'm going to the police. I'm done with it all. Time to take my fucking life back.

Verbal Warning

Chapter Twenty Six

I ignore my mum calling out to ask me to go into the lounge as I skip down the stairs and out of the front door. Her wide-eyed angry face appears at the front window as I start the car. Her fists bang at the glass and she looks right at me, demanding I go back inside. No, mummy. I promise that this is the last lunatic act that I'm going to commit, but it's something I need to do. Then I'll have some degree of closure.

I know where Barry lives. It's a shitty part of town where there's just rows and rows of shared houses. Rooms and bedsits. It's on the bus route to the college, so you get plenty of students living down there alongside the middle aged divorcees and benefits people. I once took Danny to pick some weed up from Furnivall Street after work. He said his uncle had lived down there for a while after his auntie had kicked him out. They get everything included in the rent, all the bills and stuff, I mean, but they get next to zero choice in who they live with. It's not for me, that life. Would I trade my current position with one of the tenants though? Absolutely. Come on in, sit yourself down over by the soul consuming humiliation and fanny parasites. Mind the homicidal stalker and crushing paranoia, they're not expected to be here much longer. Please, don't encourage the hilarious but unwanted nickname. If you need me I'll be waiting three days to get a go on the washing machine over at your house,

After Call Work

in the queue behind whoever else lives there, stinking of damp because I can never get anything dry.

My phone rings constantly as I drive over there. Alternating between my mum and dad attempting to speak with me. To talk me out of confronting the big weirdo. Then the texts start. Please answer your phone. We're worried. Don't do anything stupid. We love you. Please pick up. I don't want to. I can't. They'll bring a reality to what I'm doing that I can't handle right now. I need to do this. Then Amber rings. My mum has obviously been on to her. Asking where I am and what I'm doing. Amber doesn't know though. Not really. I need to be strong. I ignore her calls too.

Outside Barry's house I'm hit with a realisation that I've been here before. The guy that Danny bought his weed from lives here. As if. Barry lives with a dealer. If he knows then I bet it's blowing the weirdo's mind. He harasses HR if somebody's wearing trainers. A real life drug dealer in his house must be doing his head in. I pull out my phone and type a message to Barry. Come outside, we need to talk. Circle, tick, profile picture. Bouncing circles. **Outside where?** From the car I see a curtain twitch upstairs. I tell him his house. I tell him maybe I've come to be a beautiful elf. Circle, tick, profile picture. I can't. I ask why. Circle, tick, profile picture. **Please leave.** I get out of the car and lean against my window as I look up at the house. There's another twitch at the curtains. Fuck this. I walk to the house and knock at the door. My phone buzzes. **Please leave, it isn't safe for you.**

Verbal Warning

PART THREE

BARRY

After Call Work

MONDAY

(SIX DAYS EARLIER)

Verbal Warning

Chapter Twenty Seven

It's five hours after I first messaged her and she still hasn't read it. I sit with my laptop on that same screen. The messages on one side and my timeline on the other. Somebody I talk to in a WoW forum posts an image of their latest gear. It's a low level shield for their alt. An alt is another character that you're building up, as well as the most powerful and skilled one you have, which is your main. For example, my Priest is my main, he's maxed out on levels and has full epic gear, there's not a lot I can do to make him better. BerserkerBarry is my level eighty nine warrior. BlastedBarry is my warlock, he's level ninety one. When we weren't raiding or doing dungeons, I would take one of my alts and grind some random match instances for XP, or experience points. I click to like their image, and comment that I have the same thing for my Night Elf. They like my comment but don't respond. All the while, Penny does not read my message. I wonder if she's seen the comment I left, defending her. I wonder if I've crossed a line in some way, but we're good friends now. Friends defend friends. I message her.

As your friend I couldn't help but leave a comment Penny. These people are trolls. Steven will pay for what he's done to you. Please talk to me.

I watch it be delivered but not seen, and I watch it stay unseen. She needs to know that there's somebody on her side. I message her again.

After Call Work

You don't deserve what they are doing to you. I'm on your side and only your side. Friends stick together. I'm thinking of you hun x

I wasn't sure about saying hun and leaving a kiss as I wrote them, but they're there now. I stare at the one sided conversation between me and my beautiful nobody. She still doesn't know how much I care for her. But then what if she reads that last message and thinks I'm trying to move too fast? What if she's not at the kisses stage yet? What if I've just blown it? That x pumps and pulsates off the screen in my vision. I think I've just ruined my one true friendship with the loveliest girl alive. I feel sick. I can't keep staring at it because it reminds me what a blumming screw up I am. I close the lap top and put it on my bed. I leave my bedroom to go to the toilet but the bathroom door slams shut as I reach it.
"Oh, for God's sake," I say, too loudly, because the door swings open again, and the drug addict's face looks out at me. His eyebrow with the ring in, and three lines shaved out of, raises and he sneers at me.
"What did you say? Cunt?"
I splutter as I try to respond.
"You think there's only your fat arse that needs to shit?"
That funny smell pricks at my nose from here. The smell of drug addiction and blumming scumbags. I should be careful in case he has a syringe full of drugs that he's going to stab into me and turn me into a drug addict too. I shake my head.
"Sorry, I didn't mean to," I say, "I was just."

Verbal Warning

He steps out of the bathroom and toward me.
"You gonna tell Mandy on me again? Tell her I'm doing coke in the shitter?"
"No, that was," I say.
"That was you being a nosy fucking grassing cunt," he interrupts, "get back in your room, you dopey fat prick. You can take your shit when I say you can, alright?"
He's right in my face. His breath smells like poo and smoke. In my mind, I'm grabbing hold of the ring in his eyebrow and tearing it out, pushing it down his throat with two fingers, choking him. Watching his eyes bulge out of his head as he tries to suck air in. In reality, I'm stepping away from him slowly, disappearing into my room, falling to the floor, and crying. At the other side of the door I hear laughter, and the drug addict calling me a pussy.

The bathroom door slams closed. I hate it here, and on Wednesday I fully expect to have no job so I will have no money to pay my rent. They're going to stitch me up, like they do to everybody whose face doesn't fit their idea of the perfect agent. The perfect agent doesn't exist though. That's why in the months that I've worked at TeleWeb, I have had at least ten new starters listen in to me while they were in training, and of those ten, nobody still works there. They keep bringing new people in, but do nothing to keep those of us who actually want to work there and do a good job. The only people that are treated fairly are those who are friends with managers, or those who open their legs to the right people and will keep on opening them like loot chests in Azeroth's many dungeons,

After Call Work

right until there's nowhere left to go. Lorna. Those of us whose only ambitions are to do a good job, but don't fit the profile, they find a way to get rid of us. They call it managing somebody out. I've heard Darren say it to Zena before. He was going to manage somebody out. First, it's an informal chat about whatever, then a verbal warning, then it goes to disciplinary. From there it's final written or dismissal. If they want to manage you out, it's dismissal every time. If they want to manage you out they'll find a way to twist whatever you did and charge you with gross misconduct. There's never any consistency, unless you're somebody they want to manage out of the business. You've seen it with that blumming Steven. He can arrive late, wear trainers, speak to girls like a pervert rapist, swear as much as he likes, and take as long as he likes on his dinners and breaks. What happens to him? Nothing. I come back late from lunch three times? I'm sacked. It's not fair, and the most frustrating thing is that it will never change.

I didn't mean to be so forward. I'm sorry. If you tell me to go away I will. I won't bother you ever again.

I don't put any kisses on this one. I need her to know that I'm not like Steven. I'm not like the other boys that I have heard she has stupidly let have sex with her. Boys who have all wriggled out of the woodwork to confirm Steven's claims that she loves a rim job. I'll forgive her any and all of those times. She was probably drunk and she didn't know what she was doing. That can be the only reason a girl like Penny would have such a horrible past. She needs a friend

Verbal Warning

like me to look after her and make sure she doesn't make the mistake of letting these people take advantage of her when she has been drinking. I Googled rim job. I don't want to talk about that. It's dirty.

I'm sorry if I offended you Penny. I just want to treat you like the princess that you are. Goodnight my beautiful friend. Sweet dreams.

I press send, and with a heavy heart I shut my browser down. I get a stab in my chest when Penny on her hands and knees on the beach smiles at me from my desktop wallpaper. I know every inch of this picture. The tiny image of one of her friends taking the picture, reflected in her sunglasses. The young child sitting on a sun lounger with both hands wrapped around the lollipop they have in their mouth. The father of the same child, lifting his own sunglasses up to stare at Penny on the towel as his wife looks to the waiter with a tray of drinks. The four boys in the distance playing football. I know the exact shapes and locations of the three clouds in the bright blue sky. I know the sliver of glowing sheen along Penny's thigh as the sun reflects off the sun cream on her stunning body. I know the curve of her back as her skin disappears beneath her black bikini bottoms. I know all of it. I close my laptop, and I take a sip of the orange cordial at the side of my bed. I slide my head between the two pillows in my single bed, and I cry myself to sleep.

After Call Work

Chapter Twenty Eight

I'm in Stormwind City and there is word on the trade channel that there is a maxed out Rogue Orc using its invisibility skills to stalk the Alliance city streets, killing anybody that crosses its path. It's unconfirmed but the word is that the Orc comes from the number one player versus player guild on our server. They are as sneaky as they are ruthless, the same as any efficient Rogue. I hate Rogues. They move through our world unseen, and when we least expect it they will stab us in the back, and disappear into the shadows, leaving their poison in our veins. They have no conscience. They are only out for themselves. Add to that, it is an Orc. The ugliest of all the races. Monsters among men.

I want to stop it, but I can't fight it alone. I'm a healer. I work to close the wounds of my allies, not open those of my enemies. The tanks and the damage dealers are best equipped to deal with this. But I'm compelled to climb aboard my epic steed and offer my assistance. We gallop with haste to Stormwind Keep from the Mage Quarter, past the Trade Quarter along the side of the crystal clear canal. As my trusty steed stomps, hooves clattering against the stony floor it happens. The Orc is mounting an attack. From the heavens come more. On their dragons' backs they dive into our city. Blood Elves, The Undead, Taurens and Goblins. Our city is under attack. I watch on helplessly as they tear apart the guards that patrol Stormwind Keep. Without mercy they destroy the very people who are

Verbal Warning

supposed to keep our monarchy safe. They move into the Keep and I follow them. They cannot touch me because I haven't attacked them yet. The Orc Rogue turns to me as its allies tear the place to pieces.
"Kek," it says. I know that this is Hordish for LOL. It is laughing at me. "Kek."
All around me Alliance Humans and Dwarves and Night Elves are slain. Still I am too fearful to attack. I am not strong enough to take them. A Tauren Warrior uses Devastate and draws the guards to him. They are powerless to his skills in drawing aggro. As soon as they do, a cursed fire rains down on them from a Warlock's deadly magic. The fallen soldiers fade into nothing and the Horde army advance into the Keep. They're here for our king. This must not happen. I call upon my guild to help. We must halt their advancement upon our monarchy. The city will surely die without them. My guild are otherwise engaged. VoraciousVixen is farming motes in Outlands, AndGrenade is tanking in Auchindoun. MoneyCigs and JinglyDips, our twins, are duelling in Dalaran. Nobody will make it in time to stop them. All around me Alliance corpses fade and respawn somewhere else. This is a losing battle. I move ahead of them into the Throne Room to warn our king, but he is not there. King Varian Wrynn does not sit in his throne. In his place is the most beautiful Night Elf princess that I have ever cast eyes upon. She has long and elegant pointed ears which peek seductively through her immaculate brown hair. Her unfeasibly green eyes sparkle at me with her smile. Beneath her perfect face she wears a tiny black bikini which barely covers her wonderful breasts and lady bits. She knows not the

After Call Work

imminent danger she is in.

"My lady," I say, "you must retreat, for a Horde army is almost upon you. A salacious gathering, led by an Orc Rogue."

"Ah," she smiles, stepping down from her throne, "I've been expecting him."

This marvellous and untouched creature before me pulls from nowhere a white towel, and places it on the floor. Behind me more and more of the Alliance are slain. Fire pours down from the sky. The inflicted scatter in fear. Before me, my princess drops to her knees and lowers her hands to the floor. The curve of her back as it disappears beneath the scant black cotton is as familiar as it is irresistible. My eyes lick at her glowing white skin. I move toward her, powerless to her charms. My hand reaches to her face, but she is impossible to touch. From nowhere, the material of her bikini is pulled down around her legs.

"Here he is," she whispers as she bites her lip, "my Rogue."

Her face twists in a grotesque smirk of pleasure as she begins to jolt forwards on her knees. I cannot watch this. My princess being sullied by an invisible and untouchable force. It is as I turn away that her true name is revealed to me. Princess Rim Job Crabs Girl.

"Oh, God. Debase me with your Pork Sword of Immovable Lust, enchanted with plus eighty Filth, you dirty green monster," she gasps, "you there, Priest. Show me attention. Bless me with the Spell of Insatiable Desire. I demand it of you."

I cannot help myself. I cast the spell. Around my princess the Horde gather. They have their willies in their hands. My princess moans in pleasure. Leave her

Verbal Warning

be, I cry, but they do not understand my foreign tongue. They begin to mock me. Kek, they say. Kek. A rage builds up inside me that I cannot control. Kek, kek, kek. Then I strike. The Rogue Orc takes my weak force with ease. My enemies no longer sully my princess. I am no longer untouchable to them. They murder me in less than a second, and as my corpse fades to nothing, they turn their attention to my princess. My beautiful Night Elf princess. The last sound I hear as I fall into oblivion is my princess ask for somebody to put it in her mouth.

After Call Work

TUESDAY

Verbal Warning

Chapter Twenty Nine

I gasp awake. The digital clock says that it's just before five in the morning. My belly hurts from needing a wee. The image of Penny as a Night Elf in my dreams has stamped itself all over my brain and won't go away. The way she was. That's not her. She's just a mixed up girl who has been taken advantage of too many times. I know who the Orc Rogue was. I hate him. In the dark, the vision of my princess on her hands and knees in my favourite picture no longer has that same beauty. It's spoiled by the Penny of my dream. She doesn't smile so innocently anymore. Her pose is not something that was captured as she got to her feet on the beach. Instead, she is inviting men to come and take her. She is inviting me. To put my thing into her. No, no, no. She isn't. She isn't inviting anybody. Stop it. His poison is in me. He entered my dreams the same way he entered Penny and now he has left his disease in me. I love Penny, as a friend. I'm not like the rest. I'm not. He won't win.

It's about thirty minutes before I give in to my need to wee, as my thoughts and my aching belly don't give me any hope of falling back to sleep. The house is silent, and for once the bathroom is empty. I put my bum onto the cold toilet seat and push my bladder. The wee splashes out and I can feel the pain splashing out with it. The relief is great. Sometimes, it's almost worth the pain of busting for the toilet for that moment of relief. Suddenly something doesn't feel right. It's my legs, they're wet. My socks too. I moan in

After Call Work

frustration, as it becomes clear that most of my wee didn't go in the toilet. It has gone through between the toilet and the seat and all over my legs, my pyjama bottoms and my underpants and socks. I wasn't paying attention. I step out of my clothes and look down at the dark yellow puddle that runs along the cracks in the floor tiles. Usually, I'd clean it up but why should I? Nobody else in this house would. I bundle up my clothes, trying not to touch the bits that have wee on them, and I go back to my room as quickly as I can, in case somebody comes out and sees my bum. As I close my door I hear the creak of footsteps above me. The drug addict. There is a thump thump as his door closes, and more as he moves down the stairs. The bathroom door slams shut. He doesn't care that anybody else lives here. There is the loud, continuous deep sloshing of his wee hitting my wee in the bowl, then it stops. Then his voice. Then his voice even louder.

"You dirty fucking shits," he cries out. I smile. Sometimes the smallest, most insignificant victory is enough. In those four words, screamed out by a drug addict, high off his face on cannabis, Steven Weller, the Orc Rogue that ruins my dreams, becomes just a fraction smaller. The drug addict enters the hallway from the bathroom, no cares for the fact that it's five thirty, and screams out that whoever weed on the floor is going to have their necks pooed into after he tears off their heads. He doesn't use the words wee or poo. I hold my breath. The floorboards creak outside my bedroom as he steps gently to the door. The brushing sound of him pressed up against it. I almost cry out in alarm when he tries the handle, but I press my hand against my mouth. He can't get in. My door is locked. The floorboards creak some more as he moves away and back up the stairs to his own room. He actually tried my door handle! I should tell Amanda, the landlord, but I know that it isn't worth the trouble it would cause. He would make everything ten times worse for me. A hundred times worse.

I pull my laptop up from the floor and for the first time in almost a week I load up World of Warcraft. BlessedBarry is fully recharged. I am in the Mage Quarter of Stormwind City. I get an awful sense of deja vu, as I am in the same place as I started in my dream. To be absolutely certain that this is not all some awful dream within a dream I summon my dragon and glide over the pale grey city to Stormwind Keep and find our king. He's there, King Varian Wrynn, in some continuous loop of artificial intelligence conversation with the other Non-Player Characters. There is no princess of Stormwind. At this time of the day there are very few people playing, mostly just insomniacs and people from other countries who are a couple of hours ahead. Nobody does raids at this time. I'm the only one from my guild online, although Jammin from my friends list is around. He's always on, and everybody knows him. His real name is Benjamin. He has eight maxed out characters on Alliance, and another six on Horde. He knows the game inside and out. Jammin is talking to the whole city on the trade channel.

Jammin: *WTS sexy times 3g*
Jammin: *LF leatherworker for bad ass gimp suit*

After Call Work

Jammin: *Whose bummed there epic steed? I have*
Yuriko: *STFU dude*
Jammin: *YOU STFU*
Yuriko: *U 1st*
Jammin: *Want to fight?*
Yuriko: *I'm lvl 32 pick on somebody ur own size*
Jammin: *Get ur main*
Yuriko: *Get a life*
BlessedBarry: *You bored Jammin?*
Jammin: *Yup. Long time no see dude*
BlessedBarry: *Long story lol*
Jammin[whisper]: *Tell me youre long story*

So I do. In bite sized chunks of writing, I tell him everything. For the first time in my life, I share my pain. Not in the same way I'm telling you. You don't know it all, but since you're here and looking over my shoulder it's not a secret anymore. I start at the beginning, about how my mum and dad don't call me, and how I stopped calling them since they don't answer my calls anyway. About how my sister gets everything on a plate and about how I'm the weird one. I don't make friends very easily because I say and do things that other people don't understand. I say how I'm in masses of debt because I really don't feel grown up enough to handle bills. I wasn't raised and taught anything, I was born and then fed until I was old enough to be told my parents were moving to a smaller house. One with only two bedrooms, for them and one for my sister. I moved into a shared house at sixteen and lived with a bald biology teacher who wore Spiderman underpants every day. The radiators

Verbal Warning

always had at least one pair on them, but usually four or five. His name was Phil and he was arrested for murder last year. At the house was a Greek girl named Amelia who had thick hairs on her hands and up her arms. She once got drunk and showed me her lady bits when I told her she was pretty, after some boys who hung around at the bus stop in front of the house made fun of her moustache. When Jammin asks about how hairy it was down in her underpants, I tell him very. He doesn't say much as I tell him I moved from shared house to shared house, leaving each one in the middle of the night with my laptop and my clothes when I fell behind with rent. He swears when I tell him about how I tried to kill myself because I'm being bullied, that's right, bullied, there's no other word for it. Bullied by Steven, bullied because the managers at the call centre I work at for not much longer treat me like a Death Knight in a world of Humans. Bullied by HR who refuse to take my complaints seriously. Bullied by customers who see me as a second rate citizen. He laughs when I tell him how my coping mechanism when Steven makes his nasty comments is to anonymously destroy the life of a man who was rude to me. The same as somebody would have an elastic band around their wrist. Jake Kilner is my wrist. Then I tell him how I think I've just ruined my one shot at true happiness, because a girl I think I am in love with, the reason I have not visited Azeroth for so long, won't respond to my messages. I say I know she is going through a tough time since her email went viral after she caught sex lice from that blumming creep Steven, but I wish she'd let me in. I could protect her. Then I say that's it. I'm back in Stormwind

After Call Work

because I need to feel like somebody needs me. I need the familiar.

Jammin[whisper]: *Holy shit! You know Rim Job Crabs Girl?*
BlessedBarry[whisper]: *She's my best friend and my soul mate*
Jammin[whisper]: *You lucky bastard, she's gorgeous*
BlessedBarry[whisper]: *She really is*
Jammin[whisper]: *And she got crabs off a dude whose bullying you?*
BlessedBarry[whisper]: *Yes*
Jammin[whisper]: *So lets take him down, WoW style. Im a warrior IRL, I can help. Ive had my blades enchanted by a voodoo master whose grandma is from Haiti*

I don't even think twice. I ask for his email address. To meet a real life warrior with enchanted blades by an actual voodoo master is exciting in itself, what's most exciting is that he's willing to help. Whatever I have to do for it to mean Steven will suffer then I will do it.

By half past seven he's saying goodbye for a few hours, he needs to eat and nap. He says real life warriors can get by on a single hour of sleep a day, and even then it's a self-induced coma that they can come out of, fully alert, at the first sign of a threat. It sounds like hard work, but I guess you have to have something special. He said he could tell I had a good heart and I would make a great real life healer if I

Verbal Warning

focused. He said that the attack on Steven would show the kind of courage a person could summon when it really mattered. The last thing he took was my address. This is happening. Steven Weller is going to get what's coming to him.

After Call Work

Chapter Thirty

I can't help thinking that you're ignoring me. It's okay. I forgive you, that's what friends do. I wanted you to know that Steven won't be able to hurt you anymore. I'm dealing with it. You'll talk to me.

I left Azeroth soon after Jammin did, and went back to Facebook to check for something from Penny, but there was nothing. I did think about sending an email to her work address, but I don't think it would help my case when I go to my hearing tomorrow if I've been sending things to business emails from a personal one. They're very strict about that. With people like me. I genuinely believe that Steven could send a whole folder full of viruses that infect the entire TeleWeb network, then stand on Patrick's desk swearing and shouting that he'd done it, and he would not get so much as a verbal warning. If I sent Penny an innocent message of support then it would only be used as more evidence that I broke the rules. I won't give them ammunition. I need the job, even if I don't like it. I have a plan though. They can do what they want, but I am going to appeal the decision. I'm taking my notebook, with all of the mean things that have been said to me, and the rules that have been broken, and I'm going to share them all. Telling Jammin about my life felt like relief. Like an awful ugly weight lifted from my shoulders. I've never had anybody listen to me and let me get it out without interrupting me to call me fat or stupid before, and it felt like when I have a chest cold and there's rattling in my throat, and one

Verbal Warning

big cough shakes it loose. Tomorrow is my chance to spit it out. There will be no off the record. It will all be written down. They will get copies. That's what I need to do today, type it on my computer and go down to the library to print it up.

I don't know what to do with myself while I am suspended, it's so boring! If you are at work today would you please tell them I miss you all.

This is lies. I miss her and her alone. Her face, everything inside and beneath her head. There is still that edge that I don't like, though. The one from my dreams. The ruined holiday picture that once had a million other meanings but now represents a girl who needs psychiatric help, and a good friend who loves her.

This song reminds me of you. I love Adele. Her voice is so powerful.

I think Penny would like Adele's music, if she hasn't already heard it. The lyrics and the raw pain in them. They come from a place deep in her heart and she opens herself up for us all to see and hear the emotion inside of her. She is an inspiration, not just to women who have had their hearts broken by people like Steven, but to the nice guys. If we're patient and we can prove we're prepared to fight, then a woman like Adele or Penny will eventually find the space in their hearts to love us back. What I'm doing, with this thing with Jammin, getting Steven back. This is what fighting looks like. This is what willingness to do

After Call Work

anything for love looks like. Penny will see that, and she will be mine.

I wish you would read my messages. I love you to the moon and back.

I don't think it's ever too soon to use the L word. If you feel it then say it. What if it's your last chance to? What if, touch wood, you were hit by a car at a pedestrian crossing and never had the opportunity? This is my first experience of the beautiful feeling of knowing that one person who would make you happy for the rest of your life. I could be Penny's too, if she would only read my messages.

I check on Jake Kilner. He's been quite quiet since I reported him as a paedophile, apart from to let the world know he has told the police. He said that I better hope they catch me before he does. I'm not scared. I've covered my tracks. And anyway, they're not interested in cyber bullying. If they even did bother to take Jake Kilner seriously, then the people on Facebook will only say they should be spending the tax payer money on catching real criminals, instead of people like me with too much time on my hands. I do have a lot of time on my hands. An email comes from Benjamin Cockfoster just before lunch. It takes a few seconds to register that it's Jammin. He says he's bought his railway ticket for Thursday. He asks that I meet him at the station. He asks how many buses to my house from there. He says he has his warrior kit bag already packed. He asks if my floor is firm. He says warriors need a firm floor to rest on to remain fully

Verbal Warning

alert. At the end, he says PS. If any epic gear drops from this end-of-level boss then he would like first refusal. I tell him I'll meet him. There is one bus. I ask him what a warrior kit bag contains. I say yes. My floor is firm. The carpet is down to the thread. At the end, I say PS. He can have any gear that drops, I just need the boss for my achievement. After this, I will be BlessedBarry: Bully Slayer.

It helps, thinking of this as role-playing, in case you thought I was mad. Don't judge me. Please. Benjamin Cockfoster is the real thing, a true life trained warrior. I'm a fraud, but I know that this is my chance to show the world I won't be pushed around anymore.

Are you ignoring me? I don't know, I can't be sure because you have to read my words to ignore them. I love you, Penny Clarke.

I don't know what I'll do if she ever actually responds. It feels like I've been without her for so long, when I actually only saw her yesterday. That's a good thing. Absence makes my heart grow big and full with a fondness I would die for. I look back at the messages I've sent to her. Would she think I was crazy or would she see how I truly feel for her?

I'm going to leave you alone now Penny. I'll message you again when it's done. I love you with all my heart. Xxx

I do leave her alone. I turn off Facebook and I decide to type up my notes for tomorrow's meeting. I open

After Call Work

up my notebook at the beginning. It starts on my first day on Darren Perry's team after I came out of training. That's how long he's been doing it.

Verbal Warning

Chapter Thirty One

January 4th

09:02 Steven Weller to Darren Perry - You drew the short straw getting that fat c**t on your team Daz Pez, he stinks like shit.

Two minutes. That's how long it took him to start with me. I'd had two weeks of a safe training room, and the people I sat with when they had us listening in to live calls were all very nice. Brenda was great. A hard woman who spoke her mind. She stopped talking to me after I accidentally had her knitting needles taken away by HR. I had been taken in by the security of it all. Even on the Grad Bay I was able to put my hand up and ask for help. But then I was uprooted and dumped on Darry Perry's team. He weirded me out from the start. He had really long fingers. He was popular with the other managers and he was patient with me to begin with. Then he started to lose his cool and give me looks that said he wanted to kill me whenever I said his name, or he would roll his eyes and not even hide it. It wasn't professional and it wasn't nice. And he always, always let Steven say and do anything he wanted. You'll see.

After Call Work

09:06 S. Weller to me - Have you ever thought about using water and soap?

Once he had said some out loud things, he started to whisper stuff. Hurtful stuff.

09:15 S. Weller to me – It's not you that stinks, it's your clothes. Do you dry them at all before you put them on?

At this point, no, I couldn't dry my clothes properly. The house washing machine had broken and I had to wash some things at a laundrette, but I didn't have time to stay to dry them. I had to hang my clothes on a radiator that didn't work, with the window open in January. At one point one of the other people who lived in the house broke into my room just to close the window, it was that cold. I didn't say this back to him, obviously. I knew I had a smell around me, and no amount of antiperspirant could mask it.

10:32 S. Weller to me – Do you ever get a buzz off knowing

Verbal Warning

that some really fit birds are talking to you and they don't realise how f**king fat and ugly you are?

I didn't think about the people at the other end of the phone at all. They were problems to fix, but I just couldn't remember how to fix them. Steven started to laugh about me having my hand up and calling Darren's name out all of the time by the afternoon. It wasn't a good day, it was the first of many not good days, and they got worse and worse and worse.

April 1st

All day – S. Weller asked me about twenty times if I thought he liked me. I would answer no, and he would tell me he really did, he was just being a c**t for a laugh. Then he would say Haha April fool, I bare can't f**king stand you, you fat c**t.

After Call Work

I tried to stop answering him, but he was just so persistent. He would keep whispering my name until I just looked at him, then he'd asked me again. I would sigh and say no, then he would play the whole thing out, exactly the same, again. The look in his eyes, like he hated every bone in my body, and I really didn't know why.

April 5th

11:36 I have just left the HR office to complain about the bullying. They say I have to make a formal grievance if I want to do anything about it. They said the last part with a sigh, like they were basically saying they couldn't be bothered. They said to go away and think about whether I really wanted to go through the hassle of a grievance procedure, and whether it was

Verbal Warning

something I wanted to seriously get involved with.

This is typical of any of my visits to the HR office. I don't know what they actually did. It was three women who the managers went to before they decided to sack somebody. The same as will happen to me tomorrow. The three woman who hate me and two managers who hate me will decide whether they want me to stay and work there after tomorrow. I know I'm not the smartest man out there, but I am not stupid enough to think I still have a job by the end of the week.

April 6th

12:30 D. Perry took me into a room to talk to me about my behaviour in the HR office yesterday. He told me I needed to control my temper. He asked if I needed help. It wasn't about the bullying at all. Everything has been twisted away from the fact that S. Weller is making

After Call Work

my life a misery. D. Perry told me, before we went back onto the call floor, that it was my probation hearing tomorrow, so I needed to think about whether this was the environment for me.

That was the day that I stopped really trying. I did still do my duty as a good employee, sticking to the policies and procedures and reporting those who don't, but I was never hopeful of anything happening, ever. I kind of got even more introverted from then on, and I saw how they all are with each other. There are the managers who go out for cigarettes with Patrick, like Darren, and Zena, they are his favourites. Then those managers have their favourites who go out for cigarettes with them, whether they smoke or not. Those favourites do the floor walking when it's needed. Apart from Tony. He's not liked by many people but he's very ambitious and won't let anything stand in his way.

13:57 S. Weller to me – I can't believe you reported me to HR,

Verbal Warning

you grassing fat c**t. Make a grievance. I dare you.

14:01 S. Weller to me – You thought it was s**t before, I haven't even started with you.

14:04 S. Weller to me – What do you call a grassing fat c**t with no PC? Barry f**king Brown.

At this point I was on hold to the support department in Egypt that gets very busy at that time of a day, with a customer on hold. He leaned over and held his finger over the power button on my PC base, completely switching it off. I pressed the button and clicked to not open it in Safe Mode. I was halfway through logging my computer back on when the support department answered my call, and asked for an account number I didn't have because it was on my computer before Steven switched it off. I had to put them on hold to go back and get that information, and when I did, Steven leaned over and ended the call with the Egyptian, so I was right back at the start. The customer made a complaint about me. I didn't say Steven did it, because

After Call Work

management were accusing me of having a problem with him. What could I do?

May 3rd

It was my second probationary review today. They have extended it again because D. Perry doesn't think I can handle objections as well as other people. Julie on Alyson's team has had thirty manager calls this week already and they don't say anything to her because she's Zena's mum. It clearly states in the Retaining Equality Policy, number five, point two. No employee will be treated more fairly or unfairly than other employees in identical situations unless there is a valid

Verbal Warning

and fair reason for doing so. A case may be made by the employee to have special dispensations made, and a written certificate must be presented for these requests to be validated. I don't think Zena's mum has presented a certificate that says she is allowed to shout at customers who don't understand what she's talking about. This is a clear failure to adhere to company policies and procedures.

I hope you see now why I was so desperately miserable, and why I tried to end my life. I wouldn't do it again though, Penny has appeared to me from the darkness as a shining light of hope that not everyone is as mean as Steven, or as led by obvious favouritism as Darren, or ignorant if they have no use for you as Lorna. She arrived in my life at the perfect moment, and she, Penny Clarke, is my angel. I am going to clear her path of destructive obstacles and when I have finished, she will love me back.

Verbal Warning

WEDNESDAY

After Call Work

Chapter Thirty Two

So this is it. My inevitable fate is here. I'm sitting in the lobby of TeleWeb, with my notebook in one hand, and a new pay as you go smartphone I got from Tesco on the way here in the other. It only cost twenty pounds, which really surprised me. I never had a phone before, because nobody answers my calls anyway, but I need to know that I can see Penny when I'm not at home. If she needs me but I don't know until I get to my laptop then I could let her down.

I'm not messaging her as often now, as I said I would give her space, but this morning I had to tell her that her friend, Amber, was a bad influence. If she keeps getting led astray then she will never break the chains of her self-destructive nature. When she is mine I will not let her drink so much, I will show her that a life can be fun without alcohol and drugs in it. I will start a Night Elf character when I get home, for her, so that she doesn't have to go through the hassle of the low level quests. I will give her the same lovely wavy brown hair, and the same lovely sparkling eyes. She will not be Princess Rim Job Crabs Girl. She will be PrincessPenny, if the name hasn't already been taken. As if on cue, the horrible Amber girl comes in through the front door, alongside another girl. She catches my eye very briefly and her hand goes to her mouth. She laughs loudly and turns to the girl and mutters something. They both look to me and laugh again, then they disappear through the turnstiles.
"Bazza! Lock up your teenage daughters everybody,

Verbal Warning

it's the walking sex crime! "
I feel my heart stop and my blood run cold. I don't look up as his feet come into my eye line, and his shadow darkens my space.
"I heard you were stalking Penny" he says, then sits down beside me, "I bet it burns like fuck that even a slag like her won't even touch your manky cock."
Because I know Steven Weller is going to die, there is no longer a rigid fear, but just being near him, I'm tense.
"Don't talk about her like that," I say, "I'm not stalking her. She's my friend."
"She's seen all your messages, I heard, she's just ignoring you." He slaps a hand onto my knee and pushes himself up from the sofa as Jim and Alyson come to the lobby. "That shit travels fast, Bazza, you fat rapey cunt."
Steven walks away, patting a hand onto Jim's shoulder as he passes and nodding a hello. My phone vibrates a notification, and I pull it out, my deflation turns to elation as I see it is from Penny. She has finally messaged me! I smile as my skin prickles with joy and I can't help but blurt out a nervous laugh. I click to open it as Jim approaches. My eyes flicker across the lines of the message, my insides dying with each one that passes.

Barry, you need to stop messaging me. We're not friends. I requested you to stop you killing yourself, and now you're starting to freak me out. I don't know what I did for you to come on this strong. I'm going to block you, but I want you to get help.

After Call Work

You're a broken umbrella away from a killing spree.
Take care of yourself Barry.

I think my umbrella just broke.

I'm led along the corridors to where I know the Interview Room is. Lots of people I quite liked, all led along here at some point or another and then shown the door, along with their coats and bags, kindly collected by the manager who pulled the trigger. Jim tries to make small talk but I don't even attempt to try to listen to him or talk back. Penny and I aren't friends. She said we weren't friends. I'm freaking her out. What could she mean? *She* asked me to be *her* friend. She asked me. Jim opens a door and points to a chair that I sit in and he speaks gobbledygook to me, pointing at Alyson who has a pad and a pen and he asks me a question that I say yes to. Then I answer a no question. Then a yes. All she had to do was tell me at the start, then I would have known. I would have left her alone, but she copied me into that email, she cares what I think. She's beautiful. She looks great on her holidays. She is my PrincessPenny. I am desperate to message her back, but I am here, fighting for a job I will not keep. Jim talks about lateness, and asks me what impact I think lateness has on the business. My mouth says ehm, money? My brain will not stop throwing images and realities at me. Jim asks me to elaborate. I want to get my papers out and start talking about the comments and Steven, but I can't make my hands work. I don't elaborate. I just shrug. Jim asks me to tell him what happened at the canteen, the incident, he calls it. I say I didn't do anything

Verbal Warning

wrong. I have never done anything wrong, but everybody keeps on blumming kicking me down. I say I was late back because nobody would let me out of the doors, so I pushed my way through and a girl was knocked down.

"So you broke the Health and Safety at Work Policy?" Jim asks, his eyebrows raised.

"No, yes, but I was trying to not break the Timekeeping Policy," I moan. Penny is freaked out by me. I'm absolutely fine, she's making a big thing out of nothing. Jim shakes his head. He tells me that the health and safety of employees are the two most important things in any work place. I sigh. A pain is building behind my eye that I cannot help but rub. This is getting too much. I say I know I'm out of a job, so why are we going through all this? I say I didn't touch any girl up, I pushed her down by accident. I say I was doing it because I had three lates on my record already and I knew it would mean a disciplinary, to teach me a lesson. It would have been a lesson I would learn too, because I try to be a good employee, but they keep on kicking me and kicking me and ignoring bullying and running a blumming rubbish business because they give jobs to their friends.

"Could you slow down a little, please," says Alyson, clenching her fist and gasping, "I've got writer's cramp."

We sit in silence for about twenty seconds as Alyson rubs at her thumb and wrist.

"Just tell us when you're ready," says Jim, sounding annoyed.

After Call Work

Alyson smiles and nods at me. She says, okay. I don't say anything, because I've lost my thing, that spark to tell them off. I need to message Penny.
"Those are very serious allegations you're making, Barry. Do you want to rethink them?" Jim says, pointing a pen at me. I shake my head but don't say anything.
"Okay, so I'm going to just write *shakes his head* on here, is that okay?" Alyson says, looking to Jim. Jim rolls his eyes and nods.
I say they've already made their minds up, so they should go and see HR about who wants to walk me to the door. Jim frowns.
"I'm disappointed to hear that, Barry. Help me to understand why you feel this way."
I cross my arms and sit back in the chair, my chin pushed into my neck.
"Okay, so I think we're going to adjourn the meeting whilst I go and consult with HR and Operations before we return to you with a decision, so could you just wait here, please?"
I can't wait for them to leave so I can send a message to Penny. She's got my messages now, she's reading them. It doesn't matter what she said to me, she's opened a conversation with me, we can work it out. Surely we can. Jim and Alyson leave the room, and through the glass I see him shaking his head. I pull out my phone and tap out a message to Penny.

Penny, my darling. I'm sorry that I freaked you out. I didn't mean to. I've just missed you so much. I am going to kill Steven so you know how much you mean to me.

Verbal Warning

I press send. You do not have permission to send this user a message. I press send again. The same error. She blocked me. She actually blocked me. My world distorts as tears fill my eyes and my lip goes. The table that my legs are squeezed under begins to thud repeatedly as my body shakes and the tears keep coming. She's cut me off completely. All I have are the hundreds of pictures I saved from her profile.
Thunk.
The door to the room opens, with Jim coming in first.
"Are you okay, Barry?" Alyson asks, concerned. I shake my head, but don't go into it. I wipe my eyes with my sleeve and sit up. I sniff loudly, and swallow.
"So we've consulted with HR and Operations, and considering the severity of the allegation that you have openly admitted has happened, I'm afraid the decision has been made to dismiss you from the business. Repeated lates, issues with your attitude, and this most recent incident of attempted sexual assault, you aren't the kind of employee that we at TeleWeb would be comfortable in your remaining employed with the business. I hope you will understand and respect this decision."
I nod. Stand up.
"I'll escort you from the premises now, Barry. Are you okay?" Jim says.
I shake my head again. I don't say anything, and Jim doesn't ask. We're out of the room, and my head spins in the harsh light of the large pale blue corridor. Jim mutters small stuff about finding a new job, one better suited for somebody like me. I don't ask what he means by that. We're at the turnstiles and I swipe my

After Call Work

card through for one last time, and Jim takes it from me. As we get to the door and he holds out his hand and tells me good luck with everything I do in the future, I don't tell him I don't need luck, I'll have a fully trained warrior at my side by tomorrow. I don't shake his hand. Instead, I put my printed out copy of everything that has been said or done to me by TeleWeb and the people who work there. I tell him to read it. I tell him thanks for nothing. I leave.

My day passes in a haze of functioning like a robot, on autopilot, staring at Penny's message whilst I do it. I don't know how, but I manage to get home, into my room, and into my bed. I don't even remember taking the bus. Tomorrow will be better. Tomorrow is our time, mine and Jammin's. We will earn our achievements, and we will do it in style.

Verbal Warning

THURSDAY

After Call Work

Chapter Thirty Three

I sit in the small hall of the railway station, a picture of Benjamin Cockfoster on the screen of my phone from his email. He has long hair, and in it he is licking the tip of a knife. He says that real life warriors must push a blade through their tongue and not cry out in pain. He says they have similar philosophies to Shaolin monks. It all sounds very fascinating. The train rumbles into the station, and I stand, a nervous cloud of butterflies in my belly. I'm going to meet a warrior. He's instantly recognisable as he glides into the station hall. He wears large black boots, and torn black jeans. About that is a shirt with some sort of animal on it, and a flowing black leather coat. In his nose is a piercing that I hadn't expected, and a spike sticking out from the skin under his lip. He looks incredible.
"Ah, BlessedBarry, I presume," he says, smiling as he stands in front of me, his large bag on the floor. I nod nervously. He laughs and throws his arms around me. "What a delight to meet with you, Priest. I trust that you are well?"
I smile, and nod, and say I am. I say I'm sorry, I'm just a little bit nervous about meeting him.
"Nonsense," he says, "we are brothers in arms. We act as brothers. Do you know which chariot we must board to reach your home?"
"The number forty three," I say, "where's your armour?"
"My skin is all the armour I need," he says, patting his chest," but I do have further protection in my sack of many wonder."

Verbal Warning

He speaks so differently compared to other people, like a true warrior who has seen many battles. He is amazing.

On the bus to my house, he asks me about Steven. About how yesterday went. Penny. Dear sweet mixed up Penny. He tells me to focus on these injustices, to concentrate them into a Mote of Burning Rage. He says that's the first lesson any warrior will ever learn. The ability to increase his rage to add strength and resolve points when in battle. The boost could last for days. He said to be wary of the lows that came with the boost, though. A warrior must clear his mind of any negative thoughts. After battle, when the enemy is slain, he says, a Seroxat will always help. I close my eyes and I pull all of those unpleasant memories together and all it does is make me feel sick. I'm a long way from being anywhere near Jammin's level. He smiles through the strands of hair which hang down over his face, and pats me on the shoulder.
"It comes with a lot of practice," he says.

In my room, Jammin drops his bag to the floor and turns on my desktop computer.
"What's your password?"
"Penny123."
"Dude, you truly are overcometh by an unrequited love for Rim Job Crabs Girl, are you not?"
I smile, and nod.
"She makes me feel so protective of her. Even though she says I freak her out, I think she just needs to open up and feel the love I have for her."

After Call Work

"You are but an old romantic fool, BlessedBarry, let her go."
The familiar orchestral theme tune to World of Warcaft comes through the speakers and Jammin signs into his account. His world opens up, and he begins tapping away at the keyboard.
"Would you like a drink or anything?" I ask.
"No, I have a lovely elixir in my bag, thank you. I am spreading word of our union in my guild. We are all professionals. They were overjoyed when I told them we were meeting to do a quest. There is a Hunter who lives not thirty miles away from here. He asked if it was okay for him to come along, earn experience, and pick up any valuable loot. Would you have any objections to that, Priest?"
This just gets better and better. Attacking Steven with a warrior and hunter by my side. They can deal damage and I will heal them. I will try to heal them. I shake my head, no, and say I would be happy for the hunter to assist. This is a big achievement.
"Plus, he has a vehicle. That would be a valuable asset," Jammin says.
I nod my agreement and sit on the bed. Jammin tells his hunter the address and whilst we wait, I'm told that the hunter's civilian name is Melvyn Greedy, but his real name is PoonHunter. He is an expert crossbow handler. They had once completed a quest together to take down an old school teacher, that's how PoonHunter was initiated into the guild. Jammin says I could be exactly the kind of person they need in the guild. I just need to learn to focus my rage. This quest would be the making of me. Penny will not resist BlessedBarry: Bully Slayer. I ask how many quests

Verbal Warning

he's done, and he smiles, and says too many. He says he once took down a mob that jumped him one night, on his own. He said they were difficult to kill, but the loot that dropped was incredible. Everything was extremely desirable at the pawn shop. He says that if we take our enemies head on, we no longer fear them. They are ours for the taking. He says that tonight, I will cross a line that I cannot come back from. I will achieve a clarity that I could never know existed. I couldn't go back to how I was before, because I would never want to die not knowing that feeling of clarity felt like again. Jammin says he loves it, this is why he helps crusaders in need. He makes it his business to recruit for the movement.

"You must never breathe a word of this to another," he warns. I shake my head, transfixed by his tone and his language, and just the way he carries himself. Complete and utter control over everything he does, and he's my friend. Suddenly, life doesn't feel so claustrophobic. I have a guardian, who will help me free my biggest of demons. Even Penny fades away in his light.

"Thank you," I say to him, "for doing this. It means a lot to me."

"Not a worry, Priest. I would die to help a fellow Azerothian achieve the title of Bully Slayer, so it is my pleasure to be along to witness your glory."

His phone bleeps out at the same time that there is a knock at the front door. I hear the rumble tumble of the drug addict's feet skip down the stairs. I open my door to hear quiet voices, it sounds like the drug addict knows the person, but then he shouts out.

After Call Work

"What the fuck? What are you supposed to be?"
I move down the stairs quickly, toward the front door. In the doorway there is the drug addict, all skinny and addicted, and in front of him another man with a baseball cap on looks over his shoulder at what I assume is PoonHunter. He stands with brown shorts and green short sleeved shirt, underneath and big utility vest. On his back he has a rucksack. He looks very professional.
"Is it Melvyn?" I ask, ignoring the drug addict, who laughs.
"Fucking Melvyn? Are you kidding me?"
"Melvyn Greedy, AKA PoonHunter, at your service," he says, bowing his head slightly. He makes a move to come into the house, past the drug addict and his friend, but they tense up, obstructing his path. He looks at them both in amusement and then to me.
"Am I not invited into your home, BlessedBarry?"
I nod my head.
"Then I would ask that you stand down, I don't want to inflict violence upon you in your own home, sir."
"What the fucking hell are you supposed to be? What's wrong with your voice?" The drug addict laughs, slapping his friends arm, who joins in.
"Simply because I enunciate my words, does not mean that there is anything wrong with my voice, sir. I shall ask you one more time to stand down, or I shall punish you."
PoonHunter speaks exactly the same as Jammin does, the voice of experience. He never once takes his eyes from those of the drug addict as he speaks.
"Let the man past," calls out a voice from behind me. Jammin.

Verbal Warning

"Who do you think you are, coming into my house and chatting shit? Who the fuck are these people, fat cunt? I don't get a chance to respond as PoonHunter surges forward and grabs the drugs addict by the neck. With his other hand he repeatedly punches him in the nose. The friend tries to pull PoonHunter off but is downed by an elbow. As he lowers the drug addict to the ground, he speaks to him.
"If you speak with ill manner to my associate once more, or have any intention of retaliating, please reconsider. That is the only time I will ask."
The drug addict splutters that PoonHunter can eff off.
"As you wish," he says as he wraps his hands around the drug addict's neck and pulls him into the house. Jammin pushes past me and drags the friend in too. I close the door behind us. PoonHunter is on his knees, squeezing at the skinny neck. The drug addict yelps out that he is sorry, tapping desperately at the bare arm of PoonHunter, who loosens his grip.
"I'm sorry, I'm fucking sorry," gasps his victim. PoonHunter roots through the pockets of the wheezing man on the floor. He pulls out a wallet, and takes a thick wedge of notes. In his other pocket he finds some bundles of newspaper. It has a weird smell so I can only think drugs, which makes perfect sense. I knew all along he was an addict. PoonHunter puts the bundles of cash and drugs into his utility vest and steps over the two men on the floor.
"My sincerest of apologies for the unnecessary act of violence, Priest, but I will not allow an apprentice to be spoken to like that by a civilian. Would you like a share of the loot?"

After Call Work

I nod my head. I need to pay rent before long. He splits the cash three ways as we go up the stairs to my room. The drug addict and his friend are still gasping and whining on the floor at the bottom of the steps when I close the bedroom door, shutting in my two fully epic guardians. to go through the plan.

"We must go tonight," says Jammin, pulling out things from his bag. I'm overjoyed to see his helmet in his hands, the two ivory horns curling out from either side. Also from his bag, he pulls out a large furry coat with no sleeves. He pulls off his boots, and takes off his trousers, before putting his boots back on. He pulls the furry coat around his body and places the helmet onto his head slowly, closes his eyes, and speaks.
"I call upon you, spirit of the bear, to guide me through my arduous quest. Grant me the strength to take my enemies' lives without fear or mercy."
He opens his eyes and smiles at me.
"BlessedBarry, we must clothe you appropriately," he says moving to my bed and tugging the duvet out from inside of the cover. It's a plain beige cover I bought from Asda, in the basic range or whatever they have. I haven't washed it for a few months but it looks clean. Jammin tears a hole at the sewn up end, and on each edge at the same end and begins to undress me enthusiastically. I don't let him take my t-shirt off, but it feels funny when he is tugging at my belt. He struggles, but I don't stop him from trying for a while. Stop it. No. I take my belt and undo it, sliding my jeans off. He throws the duvet cover over my head, pulling it down around my body. I slide my arms through and look down at myself. It's pretty uninspiring.

Verbal Warning

"Here," says PoonHunter, passing me a length of cord from his bag, "usually I use it for trapping prey, but you can use it as a belt for the quest."
I wrap it around my body tight.
"Where does the boss live?" Jammin asks,. "Is there a post code?"
Then it hits me, right then, that I don't know where Steven lives. I've made such a basic error. I have let myself get pulled along in the excitement of it all that I didn't even bother to learn where my own target was. This is for *me.* They are here to help *me* complete this quest. But Jammin says you get a release, a moment of clarity that changes you. PoonHunter was new once. We all make mistakes, we learn from them. I just need to complete this quest with help from my new friends to gain experience. After that, I can complete quests on my own. I blurt out a post code from memory, but I don't say that it doesn't belong to Steven Weller. I don't say that. I cannot lose face in front of these people who are here to help. I tell him the post code, and he brings it up on Google Maps. It's twenty minutes away in the car.
"So the plan is simple, my brothers. I shall strike first, and I will maintain high levels of threat with Devastate. Hunter, you will fit his body with bolts. Priest, you must heal us if the need arises, but do not attack the beast. You will attract a greater threat that may be difficult to get back. Do you understand?"
I nod my head, which is filled with a million new different realities and emotions. I've just sentenced Jake Kilner to death.

After Call Work

Chapter Thirty Four

Jammin gives directions to PoonHunter as they both ride in the front of the car. Behind them, is me. Out of my depth and more than just a little scared. Jake Kilner is my punching bag. My stress ball. He is there to make me feel better. If I lose Jake Kilner then I lose that comfort of knowing that somebody is worse off than myself.
"Is everything okay, Priest?" PoonHunter asks, concern in his eyes in the rear view mirror. I say yes, everything is fine. I say I am focusing my rage. Trying to. He smiles.
"Good man, practice makes perfect," he says.

Fifteen minutes of pretending to focus my rage later, and we arrive at our destination. It's an address I have seen on Street View so many times, harbouring fantasies of doing just this, but it was only ever a fantasy. A way to squeeze some joy into my pitiful life. Jammin says that he will knock first. He will draw all of the threat, then we should join the attack. He says he wants the last thing that Steven sees to be my face. He needs to know why he died. He needs to hit the afterlife with a fear only of my face as his final emotion. He says this is the key to that moment of clarity. This won't be Steven though, this will be a man who I have tortured from afar for days. This will be me finally coming face to face with a voice from the end of the phone that was mean to me on the wrong day. I don't feel too good.

Verbal Warning

Jammin knocks at the door, his hands behind his back, holding two blades. PoonHunter squats by the fence, his crossbow trained on the door. I stand by the gate. This isn't right. I want to call out and say it isn't right, but the door opens, and standing there is a woman. She's wearing a dressing gown and looks terrible. Like she's been crying. Her face creases in confusion, and looks Jammin up and down.
"What are you-" is all she can say as her throat explodes beneath the bolt that PoonHunter's crossbow fires at her.
"Whoa!" Jammin gasps, ducking to his feet and looking at PoonHunter. "Stand down, hunter."
Jammin looks to me.
"You didn't tell us he lived with other civilians."
I don't know what to say. I stutter. Nothing comes out.
"What the- Danielle? Danielle?"
Over the body of the girl that PoonHunter has just killed, stands Jake Kilner. He's shorter than I imagined. He looks to the bloody mess at his feet and I feel sick and it all goes so fast as Jammin screams out Devastate and slices into Jake Kilner's chest with the knives. He screams Devastate again before calling out my name. He tells me to come and let our victim see his destructor. My legs move me uneasily along the path, and I hear Jammin say my name again. Then the floor rushes toward me and I hit it at speed. I hear *man down* being called out, as I fade from consciousness.

"BlessedBarry," a swirling, whirling voice says, over and over. Like an echo. "BlessedBarry."

After Call Work

I'm jolted awake in the back of the car. Beneath my chin, all over my duvet cover, as bloody hand marks and dragging stains. Up from that, I see Jammin's face beaming at me from beneath his helmet.
"Quest completed," he says loudly, splats of blood across his face. "Rise and shine, Bully Slayer."
"My face hurts," I say.
"You hit the ground with some force."
"Did you kill him?"
He grins.
"Of course."
I hold my hands to my face and cry out. Jake Kilner and his poor girlfriend. What have I done?
"What's wrong, Priest?"
I just blurt it out. I tell him we just murdered the wrong people. That wasn't Steven. That was Jake Kilner. I don't know where Steven lives. I cry. I say I'm sorry. I just let it happen. Jammin says he knows. He looked him up after I told him what I'd been doing. He didn't know what my plan was but he was happy to play along. I don't understand. I tell him we just murdered two innocent people.
"He wasn't innocent, he thought he could hide behind his telephone and acted horrifically. You were the victim. My life story is one long fight against injustice. I freed you of a burden. Am I wrong, Hunter?"
PoonHunter shakes his head and says he is not wrong, and calls him Warrior.
"We still have to complete the second boss before this is done, Priest."
He means Steven. I don't know that I can do this. I don't have it in me to keep up with these professionals. It isn't going as I had thought it would.

Verbal Warning

PoonHunter and his crossbow started it. There was so much blood. Jammin turns away from me and leaves me to cry in silence for the rest of the journey home. Those two talk to each other about the plan to take Steven and I walk on ahead up the short garden path. I unlock the front door, my hands shaking as I do it. We go upstairs to my room, but something isn't right. The door. It's splintered around the handle. It's open slightly. Somebody has broken into my room. Jammin catches my confused look and stops, but PoonHunter doesn't think twice and pushes his way through the door, still talking. He disappears into my room, and the door slams shut. A loud squeak of pain screams out, and several wet thuds follow. Swearing. Laughing. Nothing. Jammin stands, poised to launch himself through the door.
"PoonHunter?" I say.
"Melvyn's dead, you silly fat man," the voice of the drug addict says from behind the door. "You don't have a clue who you just fucked with, do you?"
Jammin looks to me, makes hand gestures. Keep talking.
"Ehm, no?" I say, I don't know what else to.
"Where's the Goth cunt in the undies?"
"Ehm, he's gone. He had to catch a bus."
Jammin moves to the door and his eyes close as he bows his head. His lips move as he recites something from memory quietly. I'm shaking my head, no, don't do it. Let's end this now. I have totally messed things up and three people are dead. If we don't walk away now then there will be four, or five, or more if the other people who live here come home. I wish I were anywhere else but here.

After Call Work

"Had to catch a bus my arse, send him in. He can join his silly mate."

"You don't need to do this," I say, recalling anything I've seen on television where there's a siege, "you can still walk away."

The drug addict laughs long and loud, then spits out that I can eff off, he calls me a daft C word. I look to Jammin. His eyes have glazed over, he doesn't look the same. He has focused his rage.

"Devastate!"

He roars out, kicks the door open, and disappears into the room. I hear his war cry over and over. Devastate. Devastate. Devastate. Then the door swings open. Behind it, is Jammin. Blood covered, and wild eyed Jammin. He grins.

"Target neutralised."

Verbal Warning

FRIDAY

After Call Work

Chapter Thirty Five

We still haven't moved from my bedroom since yesterday. In the corner, under my duvet, are the bodies of the drug addict and PoonHunter, also known in civilian life as Melvyn Greedy. Melvyn's face is an unrecognisable lumpy purple mess, after he was brutally attacked with a hammer. I couldn't look at him, when Jammin made me help to lift his body. It was nothing like in films. No gore. Just horrible purple cracked mounds in what used to be his face. The drug addict was a different matter. Jammin has torn him to ribbons.

We didn't sleep last night. I couldn't, and Jammin doesn't need to. Instead we talked, and he scoured the Internet looking for Steven's address. It wasn't going away. Jammin wasn't going away. Even when I told him to leave and I would take the rap, he said no. He had a fallen comrade to avenge.
"But you've avenged him," I'd said, "his killer is dead." He'd shaken his head and said he was completing the quest in PoonHunter's honour. Nothing I did or said made any difference. I was stuck with my warrior guardian whether I liked it or not, so we talked. Jammin has completed about forty quests, he said. He is trained in several martial arts. He said he used to be fat, and with a civilian name like Benjamin Cockfoster, he was a target for bullies everywhere. Then one day he signed up for a taekwondo class, and it changed his life. He took up more and more classes, lost weight, grew stronger. Fitter. He got some black belts. Then he

Verbal Warning

discovered that he could focus his rage when he was faced with an old adversary from his school days, and that was the day he completed his first quest. He has a storage unit full of the loot he has taken from his fallen enemies. He told me that he has committed his life to helping others in need, and he has been called a hero by many. I didn't tell him that I wished I'd never met him.

By mid-afternoon, a stomach turning realisation hits me. Not like before, not in the heat of the moment, but forgotten about when a new disaster happens. It's more something that feels like pieces of a jigsaw I don't know falling into place, and then as a final piece is clicked I understand what's happening and what the image is. It happens when Jammin tells me that the bodies of our first enemies have been discovered. I tried so hard to ignore it. To forget it had happened. Now it's here in black and white and blue and blumming red. Jammin calls them enemies, the news calls them victims. Jammin calls them quests, the news calls them premeditated killings and robberies, after the victims were previously subjected to an anonymous campaign of intense online harassment. Jammin calls us Bully Slayers. The news calls us murderers. We are murderers. This isn't a game at all. Jammin isn't a warrior. He is a deranged serial killer parading as a hero, dragging people like me into his sick activities. I'm stuck in my own home with a psychopath who doesn't see people as people at all. He sees them as mobs in a game that he is the main character of. What have I done? What the blumming heck have I done?

After Call Work

I feel my bones go cold, the blood that flows in and around them freezes. My hands shake, and it runs up my arms and into my neck. I feel so cold. My legs shiver and shake and I don't know what's happening to me. My belly tightens, and so does my throat. I can't get warm. I can't breathe. I wheeze like a dying seal as I suck precious little air in. I stumble as I rise from the armchair, attracting Jammin's attention. An echo of him asks if I'm okay. An echo of me says we're murderers. This isn't a game. He's insane. My hand reaches to one of the eight knives that swirl around on the computer desks beside the four images of Azeroth on my six computer screens. Then four of my hands hold the knives to four of my wrists. I say it has to end. It has to end. A gang of Jammins, all together, shout no. Put the knife down. Please. Don't let them win. You're so close to killing your demons. Freeing yourself.
Don't let them win. The point of the knife presses into my skin and it hurts. I didn't kill anybody, I think I say. I hope I say. It wasn't me. It wasn't me. I'm not a killer. He says I am. His face is no longer concerned. His face is angry. His voice is angry. His words cut deeper than this knife in my wrist.
"You won't fuck this up, Priest. Show some fucking balls, you fat coward."
And there it is. My weight comes into it. The one word that defines me in the eyes of others, and gives them a whole list of insults to work with. Fat. I drop the knife to the floor and sit down again. I cry. Jammin stands over me. He speaks but I'm not listening. He puts three pills in my mouth and gives me some juice to wash them down. He speaks again and this time I do listens.

Verbal Warning

He talks about how they all do this. They all panic. He says it's part of the initiation. He says it will pass. He says he knows where Steven lives. He says to sleep. The Diazepam will take care of me. He will take care of everything else. I drift away, to dreams of Azeroth and Princess Rim Job Crabs Girl.

After Call Work

PART FOUR

SATURDAY

Verbal Warning

Chapter Thirty Six

Barry

At I don't know what time, I wake up, still in the armchair. It's still light outside, so it can't be too much later. My head feels tired. Groggy. My mouth feels dry. Claggy. My eyes heavy. Sticky. Jammin is, I don't know where. My room is empty, other than the usual things. A flash of a memory strikes me hard. The corner of the room. The bodies. They're gone. For a very short moment I'm convinced that I've imagined everything, but then the blood stained carpet tells me no, everything happened. My phone buzzes in my pocket. Where are the bodies, and Jammin? I swallow. I try to swallow. The phone is in my hand. I have a message. A Facebook message. A Facebook from Penny. She misses me, she wants me as much as I miss her. She can make it all better. I eagerly open up the message.

I know what you've done.

My fingers ask, what have I done? My head hurts. The brightness in the room burns my eyes. She reads my message and responds and the room around me disappears. I lean forward in the chair and topple forward, my hands don't help to stop me. My fat stupid head hits the thin manky carpet and my fat stupid head makes the house shake. My fat stupid head twists and my stupid eyes look at the bright white screen on the phone in front of my stupid face, with three words on the blue speech bubble.

After Call Work

You've murdered him.

How could she know? There is no way she knows. Unless, Jammin? Has he set me up? Where is he? Another message pops up.

You killed him, didn't you?

It wasn't me. I killed nobody. I haven't killed anybody. I can't even kill myself, how am I supposed to have killed somebody else? I lift my fat stupid head from the floor and scoop up the phone and I tell her. *It wasn't me.*

The door opens and he walks in. Jammin. In his arms he's holding a small television and a cycle helmet. His costume confuses me, his long thin legs in the black boots. His thighs, his underpants, the shaggy coat with no sleeves that's covered in, blumming, blood. His thin long hair and Viking helmet. It confuses me. I look at my duvet cover hanging down over my fat belly. The belt that digs into my skin. What are we doing?
"Ah, sleeping beauty awakens," he says cheerfully, "you would not believe the loot that has dropped."
He puts the television down and shows me the helmet. It's a shiny black one, red on the inside.
"The Epic Helm of Greater Healing. Boosted by two hundred Intellect points. This is rare drop, Priest. Equip it so that I may see you."
I watch his face to see if he's joking but he obviously isn't. He wants me to wear the cycle helmet, indoors, as part of my stupid costume. Even though I don't want to, I reach out and take it. It's too small for my fat

Verbal Warning

stupid head but I squeeze it down on top of it and look up to Jammin's satisfied face.
"Perfect," he says, "we will make a healer of you yet."
"Where are the bodies?" I ask.
"They have respawned," he says with a smile, "PoonHunter is back in Dalaran, no doubt."
"Please don't treat me like an idiot," I say, "people don't respawn in real life. What did you do with them?"
His eyes lose their sparkle, and his cheek twitches as he stares at me through his greasy hair.
"It's better that you don't know," he says finally.
"Are they still in the house?"
"No. I moved them overnight, they will not be discovered, I can assure you."
"Overnight? How long was I sleeping?"
Jammin shrugs.
"What day is it?"
"Saturday," he says, then waves both of his hands in front of him, jazz hands, "the freakin weekend, baby."
I frown. That didn't sit right.
"What are you? Really? What are you?"
He clears his throat. Lowers his head. Watches the ground for a little while then lifts his eyes to look at me.
"You're starting to take the fun out of questing, Priest."
I've had enough. He's starting to take what miniscule bit of fun there was out of my entire life.
"Questing? It's murder, Benjamin. You're murdering other people's problems. What happened? You ran out of your own bullies to murder so you started killing other people's? Is it really that simple?"

After Call Work

"I'll remind you to watch your words, BlessedBarry. An overweight and pathetic level one Priest is no match for a maxed out Warrior. I shall force you to engage in player versus player, and you will not come out of it well, I can promise you that. I am returning to the villain's lair to see if any more loot has dropped."

I sigh. I'm stupid and even I can see the irony in my supposed protector bullying me with his words. There's no point in arguing. I won't say anything else to him. He can drag me along in his games, but he is getting nothing from me. When this is over, I will tell the police everything. He can have right now, but the future is mine. My phone vibrates in my hand. I try to ignore it, but I know it's from my beloved. She says that we need to talk, she says to come outside. I don't know what that means. I'm not sure it's meant for me. I ask her where as I check the street from the window. There's nobody there. Only cars. She says my house. Please, no. Please go away Penny. I don't want you to be hurt. I beg her to leave. From the window I see her, leaning against a car. Sweet and beautiful Penny Clarke, come to see me. To speak with me. She isn't smiling. Oh no. She is walking to the house. I tell her she needs to leave, I tell her it isn't safe. She doesn't listen.

Penny

"Barry, open this fucking door," I say through the letterbox. I see his feet halfway down the stairs. He has sandals on his bare feet.
"You need to go, Penny," he mutters.

Verbal Warning

"Fuck you, you big stalking wanker. You need to tell me what you've done to him."
His feet move another few steps. He's not wearing trousers though. As his knees come into view it looks as if he's wearing a duvet cover, or one of those Roman gowns or something. His big waist appears next, and he has a rope around his gut area.
"It wasn't me," he says, as the sight of his chest covered with blood takes my breath, "it wasn't me." He sits on the bottom step and looks at me. He's wearing a bike crash helmet on his fat head, completing his ensemble outfit of insanity.
"What have you done, Barry?"
He shakes his head, his bottom lip twitching in the mass of hair that has grown over his face.
"Nothing. It wasn't me," he says, "I'm the healer."
"Whose blood is that? Is it Stevie's?"
He shakes his head.
"Jake Kilner's," he says.
Who. The fuck. Is Jake Kilner? I drop the letterbox closed and stand up. I go faint, and a hot flush prickles up my chest and into my face. A logical explanation floats on a piece of driftwood in some Down Under sea at the other side of the world. I go back to the letterbox. I flip it open to see a boy beside Barry. He's wearing very shiny black high platform goth boots to just below his knees. Up from that are underpants with no trousers, and a brown fur gillet with no shirt. On his head and matted long brown hair is an old looking Viking helmet. One of those ones with the horns. The few clothes he's wearing are spattered with blood. His skinny face has two stripes of blood down each cheek. He stares directly at me, his hands

After Call Work

pushing their way into the pockets of his gillet.
"What are you supposed to be?" I say, before looking to the slumped and sweaty Barry. "Who's Jake Kilner? Why are you dressed up? Have you killed somebody? Where's Stevie?"
"Blessed Barry," says the other weirdo, taking his eyes from me, and pulling two massive knives from his pocket, "heal me."

I'm up on my feet and down the path when I hear the door go behind me.
"Devastate," roars a voice. I'm by my car and searching for my keys when he gets to the gate.
"Devastate," he shouts again. The man in the pants and goth boots gets closer and I unlock the car and slide in. I lock it as he stands beside my window. His narrowed eyes bore into me as he shouts over and over again. His spit splats against the glass. Then he screams out once again and pulls his arms into the air, both knives pointed away from me.
"Devastate!"
I twist the key and put the car in gear as he smacks his knife handles against the glass. I shield my face from a shower of shards that doesn't come. Instead, there's a scream. "Healer!" The crazy person with the knives screams it again and presses two very bloody and very wounded palms against the glass. I shake my head at Barry, who holds out a roll of toilet paper to his bleeding friend, and I point to my temple.
"You're fucked in the nut, mate." I point to Barry and speak extra loud, so he doesn't mistake my words for a declaration of undying love. "You're going down for this. You crazy cunt."

Verbal Warning

I press the accelerator hard and leave the fancy dress murderers behind. In my rear view mirror I see Barry in his duvet cover and sandals standing in the street and looking at me. His silly friend is doubled over, holding both hands into his fluffy coat.
I round the corner and I dial all of the nines. I say which emergency services. I say my name. I say what happened. I say weapons. I say murder. I say escape. I say costumes. I think I say Jake Kilner. I definitely say Stevie. I say blood. They say stay here. I ask if they fucking kidding me. I say I'll be at home. I say I'm going home. Then they're gone and I phone my mum. I tell her I'm sorry. I say I'm coming back. I say that I'll tell her everything.

Barry

"Heal me, you fucking imbecile," Jammin roars at me, holding out two hands, both with deep red slices through the palms, blood gushes from them, "I'm bleeding to death."
I watch his hands waving, they look quite sore.
"I don't know how," I say, "I'm not an actual healer. You do know that, don't you?"
"Don't you know basic first aid? You look like you could have been in cubs or something. Don't you dare tell me you weren't even in fucking cubs. Heal me, for fuck's sake."
"No, Benjamin Cockfoster. I won't," I say, and step away from his reach as he doubles over in pain, I've had enough. "Or should I say, Benjamin Cock*head*?"

After Call Work

It feels good. Even the swearing. I get the same kind of rush that I had when I first sent Jake Kilner a bacon sandwich. *I* have the upper hand.

"Is that what they called you? The others you murdered? Did they say you got fat from eating too much cock? Benjamin Cockeater?"

He glares angrily up at me.

"Shut up, Priest. I'm warning you."

"I'm not a blumming priest, I'm a fat stupid idiot who doesn't have a job, but at least I know what it feels like to love something. Somebody."

Benjamin laughs at me.

"Who? Crabs Girl? Did you not hear what she said? She called you a big stalking wanker. Were they the first words she'd ever said to you? You lied to me, Barry. She is nothing to do with anything."

I can win her back. He's wrong.

"Shut up, okay?"

Some people have started to appear at their doors, watching us. The other people who live in my house. Curtains twitch. I'm suddenly very aware that we aren't alone. Two boys, no older than sixteen, hold their phones up to us. Behind them they stare at the screens.

"Looking bare Game of Thrones on ketamine, fam," one of them calls out to me.

"Hey, where's your midget?"

"I'm dying, help, please" says Benjamin to the boys. They move away from him.

"Fuck off," laughs the first one, "you cut yourself up with your own blades, you're a fucking idiot, fam. You're bare going on Rude Tube, innit?"

Benjamin stands straight. Clenches his bleeding fists.

Verbal Warning

"You don't know what I can do to you, you snivelling bastards, turn off those cameras now, I demand it of you."
"Yeah, alright, the day I take orders from Lord of the fucking Rings in his undies and a fat duvet is the day I walk myself down to the tracks and throw myself in front of a train, innit."
Benjamin steps toward them, and his knives on the floor. His breathing has change. It's heavier. He's focusing his rage. That's what he calls it, but he's just getting angry. He's dangerous when he's angry.
"Please don't," I say to everybody.
"He's dangerous, he's killed over thirty people," I say to the boys and their cameras, "stop saying those things."
"It's over," I say to Benjamin, "don't do it."
He turns to me as he stands by his discarded knives.
"No, Priest. There's always a bigger fish to take you down another peg. It's never over."
The boys don't move anywhere as he squats to take his weapons. I could never outrun him, but I take a few steps back anyway. He turns to the boys, and opens out his arms wide. Still, the blood drips from his hands as they wrap tight around the blades.
"My name is Jammin the Bully Slayer, of the army of Stormwind. I serve King Varian Wrynn alongside my brothers and sisters of the Alliance of Azeroth. I regret nothing."
Benjamin swings his arms in quickly, digging the knives deep into himself. I gasp. The boys behind their cameras laugh and swear as they fall into each other. Benjamin doesn't turn to look at me at all. He coughs and whimpers, then he falls to his knees. I go into the

After Call Work

house and I walk up the stairs to my room. I sit at my computer and I write an email to her work address. I tell her I'm sorry one last time, amongst some other things that I don't really want to tell you just now. I'm tired of it all. If you want to stay and watch me die then stick around. Misery loves company. I've heard that phrase a few times in my life. Usually when Steven would sit across from me at lunch just to- Steven. Benjamin said he would take care of it. What happened? I don't care anymore. It's not my problem. None of you are my problem. I stand up and throw the bicycle helmet onto my bed. The Epic Helm of Greater Healing. What a joke. Me, not the helmet. I take the duvet cover off and loosen the rope around my belly until it falls from one hand. It's thicker than George at Asda laces. Thank you for the advice, Steven. I tie it around the hook in the back of my bedroom door as tight as I can. You know the rest.

Penny

My mum is at the window as soon as I'm pulling into the drive. Her mouth drops open in bare horror when she sees the blood. I don't even know what just happened, to be fair. That was mad as fuck. Something about Barry and a naked Goth covered in blood. Knives. He didn't kill Stevie. He said he didn't kill Stevie. What the fuck did I nearly get involved in? My mum's pulling me out of the car and taking me back to the house. She's kissing my head and closing the door behind us. My dad's in the hallway with Amber. Everybody looks concerned. My mum says I'm a stupid girl. I shouldn't have gone there. I could have

Verbal Warning

been killed.
"What? How do you know? What?"
I don't have much else to say than that just now. Amber runs forward and shows me a video that she says has gone round like wildfire. As she tells me that there were two kids in their front yard watching everything, I see me shouting through the letterbox. She says they put it on YouTube ten minutes ago and it's already had thirty thousand views. The title is GIRL SHOUTS THRU LETTERBOX... YOU WONT BELIEVE WHAT HAPPENS NEXT! It's all anybody is talking about. I watch as I run away from the house and that fucking clown in the boxers comes out shouting and waving his blades. I scream at Barry then drive off. She tells me that the kids who put the video up have said in the comments that the police are there. The naked Goth shouting at the camera, and then. Ohmagod. I push the phone back into Amber's hands and throw myself at my mum. I tell her shoulder that I'm sorry. I don't know what came over me. She hushes me. She tells me it doesn't matter. She kisses my head.
"I've not handled this very well, mum," I say, "I've been getting harassed everywhere after Stevie and everything. Barry was messaging me all the time, he said he was going to kill him. Then Stevie went missing so I looked for him. I didn't want to be responsible," I say, "I didn't want to be responsible."
"Hey, listen to me. You're not responsible for any of it. Okay? None of it."
"I still don't know what happened to Stevie."
"Forget him," she says, stroking my hair, "you need to talk to the police, though."

After Call Work

I nod into her shoulder.
"I know. I will."
"It's already on forty thousand views," says Amber, "babes, I think you're about to get a new kind of famous."

Verbal Warning

Chapter Thirty Seven

ONE WEEK LATER.

It feels weird, walking through the doors and onto the call floor, even if it's totally dead at this time. Only a handful of early morning weekend staff in who look up at me as if they're seeing a ghost. I will be, very shortly. I'm only here to get some stuff out of my locker and then tell them to shove it up their arses, really. I know, I know. Don't burn your bridges. But fuck it. This place has caused me nothing but grief. I don't ever want to put another headset for as long as I'll live.

It's been a strange few days, this last week. Even by my own recent fucked up standards. Spent mostly moving from police interviews to the news interviews that I've been allowed to do. They all want a piece of me at the minute, but I haven't been allowed to say too much about too much to the media, because of the case that's happening. They say Barry is part of a three year long investigation into a load of random unsolved murders.

The police think he was part of an online ring of lunatics that put each other up to killing people. They asked why I was there. I told them why. They asked what my relationship with him was. They asked if we'd ever shagged. You know, because they just have to ask the question. I told them I'd barely even spoken to him. I told them my relationship with him was that I had no relationship with him. They asked what Stevie

After Call Work

had to do with anything. I told them that it looked like he had nothing to do with anything. I just reacted badly to the Rim Job Crabs Girl thing, I didn't get help when I should have. I'm nineteen, going a little crazy is my prerogative. Out of interest, I said to them, have you spoken with Stevie? They said he still hadn't surfaced. Nobody had seen him at all, but nobody was reporting him as a missing person so they weren't treating it as suspicious. His silly house mate dropped the allegation against me too, which was wise of him. A guy who lived in Barry's house has been in touch, too, Allen Inches he said his name was, before spelling his surname out to me and telling me to look on Amazon for his work. He said he was a novelist who wanted my side of the story. He said he was researching for a true crime novel based on the psychopath that was living under the same roof as him without his knowledge.

Barry's dead, by the way. They found him hanged and naked. The rumour is that he went straight to his room to have himself a dirty bit of a choke wank and it went wrong. It's more likely that he just finally succeeded in topping himself. It's awful to say, but I'm glad. He was clearly too far gone in the head to come back from his own personal hell. It's a shame for the families of his victims, obviously, but a creature as tortured as Barry needs putting out of their misery. That's my opinion, anyway.

"Penny," says Jim in surprise as I approach his desk. "How are you? I mean. After."

"I know what you mean, Jim. I'm fine. As fine as can be expected, I guess."

"What are you doing here?"

Verbal Warning

"I've come to hand my notice in and clear my locker and computer out. Is that okay?"

"Uh, yes, I suppose so. Are you sure you don't want to reconsider?"

I laugh loudly and suddenly. Do I want to reconsider? Do I want to reconsider my belief that even after everything I've gone through, from the crabs and the slut shame to being almost being bare stabbed up by a gang of serial killers, that it's still all more favourable than another minute of speaking with the ignorant cunts on the other end of the phone and working for ignorant cunts who only offer leg-ups to their ignorant friends?

"I'm sure, Jim," I say. He stands up, and looks funny, like he wants to say something. I look at him, expectantly. Eventually he beckons me elsewhere and walks to the Pod. I follow him out of curiosity.

"Did Barry ever tell you he was being bullied? I mean, full on brutal bullying?" Jim asks me quietly, his eyes darting around the call floor.

"No, but it was pretty obvious. He hated Stevie. Why?"

He frowns.

"Just something he did when he was dismissed. It's been on my mind since it happened. I think we let him down badly. I'm putting evidence together to take it further. If you remember anything will you tell me, please?"

I nod. I'm not getting into any citizen's arrest bullshit, but I'll play the game. Jim's one of the good ones.

"Thanks," he says. I go back to my desk and load up the PC to clear off some stuff and send myself some things I've had stored on there, including emails from Barry to give to the police. My email account has

After Call Work

thousands of unread messages, so I search his name. There are the ones from before everything, and some others that we've both been copied in on. Tony. I will not miss those URGENT messages. Not at all. Then there's one which makes my skin crawl immediately. Instinctively I glance at Jim, who is involved in his own worries. I open the email, and my heart melts.

From: blessedbarry@hotmail.com
Subject: Goodbye

Dear Penny

I want to tell you how very sorry I am for everything that I have done. I have been a stupid idiot. I still am one. I did'nt mean for anything of this to happen, and I hate myself for what I might have put you through.

When you read this I will probably be dead. I'm sorry that I was so pushy and for making you think I was a stalker. I'm not one. I just haven't ever had a real friend before, and I thought that you could be my first one. I am not very good with people and I acted like the fat stupid idiot that I am and I scared you. And I made you mad and I didn't mean to.

I did'nt kill Steven, but it's my fault if he's dead. The same as it's my fault Jake Kilner is dead, and his poor girlfriend, and the drug addick who live's at my house. It's all my fault because I brought Benjamin Cockfoster into our lives. He's a pycopath who

Verbal Warning

pretends like he lives in computer games and does'nt see other people as people. He was. He is probably dead now too. I am sorry that you were almost one of his victim's.

Steven Weller is a bully who has spent all of the time that I have ever known him making my life hell. He is cruel and if he isn't dead then he should be.

I'm going to go and try to do what I should have done properly the first time. Thank you for offering me the gift of friendship, I am sorry again that I abussed it. Good luck with everything Penny, you are an angle.

Love from Barry. Xxx

I read it over three or four times before forwarding it to my personal email address, and then to Jim, and then to Detective Sergeant Jude Elland from the police. I close down my computer for the last time, and tell Jim I'm going. He looks up from his own computer and says he'll escort me from the premises.
"What will you do?" Jim asks as we pass the lockers, and all of the empty desks. Soon to be filled by the Saturday shift. Hundreds of people who ended up here by accident, or by necessity, but rarely by choice. People who watch others leave here for good, through eyes of burning envy.
"I'm hoping to just lie low for a bit, to be honest, Jim. This whole thing isn't going away. I just can't handle,

After Call Work

well, this," I say, waving my arms around, "I don't know how you do it."
"Might not be for much longer," he says, "it'll all be in India soon, no matter what that lying prick Martin Rose says."
"Really? That's a shame."
"Yeah. It is."
We get to the door, and I hand my pass to my manager. There's a weird moment between us where we aren't sure how to leave it. I choose to go in for the hug. Like I've said, he's one of the good ones.
"Make sure Barry didn't die for nothing, Jim," I say.
"I will," he says, "I promise."
I smile at him and say goodbye, and I walk away from the building for the last time. As my car comes into view, I pull out my phone and call Amber.
"Hey babes, you free for visit? I know it's early but I want to get bare smashed."

The End... For now.

The After Call Work story will continue in After Call Work: Gross Misconduct, coming in early 2017.

Verbal Warning

After Call Work

Afterword and acknowledgements

Here again. Thanking people for their support in my ongoing attempts to tell stories that will make you laugh, cry or vomit.

Thanks to my beautiful wife, Rebecca, and my even more beautiful daughter Delilah. You make me feel human, both of you.

Thanks to my old mucker, Mark Wilson. The ball's in your court now, cunt.

Thanks to Ben Fleat Barrozo, John Kelly, John Davies, and Neil Cocker for your preview assistance along the way.

Thanks to my six years working in a call centre for all of the material. It was a job I took to get out of a bind when I took redundancy from an old job. I ended up staying on for six years, desperately chasing a carrot that ultimately ended up rotten to its core. You just gave me four books of beautiful cynical material. So for that, thank you and fuck you, Webhelp UK, Manvers, Rotherham.

And thanks to you, whether you're a regular reader or a newbie, for picking this up and letting me entertain you. Please go and drop a review in at Amazon, if you can spell. If you can't, just go and slobber on a shoe or something. I love you.

Verbal Warning

Book Two will focus a lot more on the inner workings of the call centre, and the desperate chase for 'opportunities' that the more ambitious of its patrons will undoubtedly undertake. I hope you'll join me.

@ryanbracha on Instagram or Twitter. Ryan Bracha on Facebook.

Find me, follow me, love me.

Printed in Great Britain
by Amazon